Where Somebody Waits

Where Somebody Waits

MARGARET KAUFMAN

PAUL DRY BOOKS
Philadelphia 2013

Acknowledgments

Thanks to the following journals in which some of these stories have appeared: *Ascent*, "Ducks"; *The Marlboro Review*, "Butterflies"; *The Missouri Review*, "Ruby's Gift"; *Staples*, "Adaptation," *Kenyon Review*, "Fishing."

First Paul Dry Books Edition, 2013

Paul Dry Books, Inc.
Philadelphia, Pennsylvania
www.pauldrybooks.com

Cover design by Karen Horton

Printed in the United States of America

Library of Congress Cataloging-in-Publication Data
Kaufman, Margaret, 1941–
  Where Somebody Waits / Margaret Kaufman. —
First Paul Dry Books Edition.
    pages cm
  ISBN 978-1-58988-089-4 (alk. paper)
  I. Title.
  PS3561.A8612W48 2013
  813'.54—dc23

                                    2013022894

Contents

For my beloved, Joseph Bodovitz

Where Somebody Waits

Fishing

⁓

"Going someplace special?"

"It depends on your point of view," Ruby told the man who handed her a pair of stockings across the counter. "I'd like to use your dressing room to put these on." She smiled, and he nodded toward a curtained alcove. He'd waited on her before. He was maybe a little older than thirty, too old to be drafted off to war with the younger men she sometimes wrote letters to. He was several inches shorter than she was, maybe five feet six, and appeared solidly anchored to the floor with his shiny brown shoes and patterned socks. His suspenders were patterned, too, clipped to his light-brown trousers with a precision she found reassuring. He wore gold cuff links, and even now, at day's end, his shirt was still smooth on his slim body. He looked comfortable. She adjusted her new stockings and tucked the ruined ones into her purse. She could use them to wrap curls.

"I'm going to the tents to hear the preacher," she announced. Although Ruby had her doubts as to the power of prayer, her point of view could be summed up this way: it couldn't hurt. And what didn't hurt anybody else was mostly all right.

The man was leaning against a counter, grinning at her as she stepped through the curtain and back into the main part of the store, his chin emerging from dewlaps that reminded her of a favorite basset hound, long dead. He smiled as if he approved of her height, taking in her red pompadour, the way her hair flowed about her shoulders.

"He'll want to save you," he said, "I know he will."

Ruby looked blank. "Who?"

"That preacher, lucky dog," he said. "My name is Bubba," he said offering his hand, "Bubba Davidson. This here's my store."

"Ruby Daniels," she said shyly as they shook hands, then she laughed. "Save me? Do I look lost?"

He examined her palm as though reading her future. "You look found to me, Miss Ruby. Are you going all alone out to the tent?"

And so Ruby and Bubba went together to the revival meeting. He had paid for some of the fans people would be using, he explained, he and another Rotary Club member, the funeral director, Mr. Stevens.

"I never been out there myself," he said, "but I'd like a look at those fans. Picture of Jesus on one side, on the other, 'Shop at Davidson's,' a drawing of the store. No address. Everybody knows where we are." He looked at his watch. "Early, though. Time for a quick bite. That is, if you're not engaged."

He took her to the Blue Rock, where her friend Doris Jean raised an eyebrow over her order pad and winked at Ruby. They'd been in school together, country girls who had attended the consolidated school from even smaller towns than this one, riding the yellow school bus right through to the end of senior year because no one had cars, no one who was safe to ride with.

"You want a Co' Cola or a beer?" Doris Jean asked.

"Have whatever you like," said Bubba. "I'll have a whiskey to keep you company. You shouldn't drink alone."

Ruby nodded, puzzled. She came here often, did most of her drinking alone, didn't see why not.

"What's *alone* got to do with it?"

Bubba frowned. "Drinking is a social activity. If you're thirsty, you can drink water. But drinking needs companions." He tilted back his chair and appraised her critically. It seemed to her he was sizing her up like something he'd buy for his store. "You're a pretty young thing. You don't even know what I'm talking about. I'm talking about alone.

"I'm a bachelor, getting set in my ways. To tell you the truth, it scares me a little. Take drinking: I never have a whiskey unless I'm in company, for fear it will become my friend. I'll start to look for it, depend on it—it will always be there when I need it, and I don't want to end up blear-eyed, talking to myself. I don't permit myself to drink alone."

"I like to drink," laughed Ruby. "Any time you want a drink, you call me up; I'll come out with you, Bubba." She dropped her eyes. "Can I call you Bubba?"

He was cute, so serious-minded. She'd never thought of anybody *thinking* on whiskey, how it kept you company, but it was true, it did, and it was good company too. She mixed hers with Coke, drank it out of a Mason jar, so once she was settled on her sofa, smoothing down the chenille coverlet, she didn't have to get up again. The Mason jar held enough to get her through the evenings in her garage apartment. She decided not to tell him that. He didn't think she knew about alone.

"Everybody calls me Bubba," he was saying, "even the colored, they call me Mister Bubba. It isn't disrespectful; it's my name."

"Your Christian name? Go on."

"My given name," he said, "is Nathan. I'm not Christian. I'm a Jew."

Ruby opened her mouth then clamped her fingers over it. In a vague way she supposed she knew there were Jews in the town, but she'd never considered she might meet one. She'd heard they had horns, but suspected it was a lie. Now, so close across the table, she could see for herself, but she thought she'd offend him if she looked too closely. It angered her, such foolishness, especially in herself. She noticed he said "colored" instead of "nigger." Maybe he was a liberal. Well, that was all right.

"I've never had the pleasure," Ruby said, removing her fingers from her mouth, "but Jesus Himself was a Jew, and Peter and the apostles. Oh, shoot, I never held much with any of that business." She laughed. "If I told you what I did instead of going to Sunday School, you'd be shocked."

"Pretty as you are, it would be a sin to keep you cooped up, even on Sundays."

"We lived downriver from here. I moved to town last year after graduation. My folks were riverdippin' Baptists. I didn't hold much truck with that, so I went fishing on Sundays," she said, her laugh rippling, her fingernails flashing as she pushed her hands through her hair and tossed it back.

She wouldn't tell him about the Ferris boys, how she and Martha Nell would take off with them on Sundays. They kept an army blanket rolled up in oilcloth and cooled beer in the river. Sometimes she did fish. She liked it too.

"Fishing?" The way his voice dropped was attractive. In his face was a sense of the humor in things. "I love to fish and hunt," he said. "My mama says I love it too much, that I ought to settle down."

"I don't ever want to settle down myself if it means not doing what I like," she said defiantly. "My sister moved to Little Rock, but she didn't really want to. Now she's good and sorry."

"Would you come fishing with me?"

"Yes," she said, her chin leveled at him across the table, "yes indeed. And I gut my own fish, too."

When they got to the fairgrounds, it was growing dark. The tent was lit up all around. A litter of kittens chased each other around one of the pegs that anchored the canvas, batting at the cord. Ruby and Bubba stepped around them and through the open flap, then chose seats at the back, on the aisle.

"This way we can duck out if we don't like it," Bubba whispered. He leaned over and picked up one of the cardboard fans that lay on the folding chairs. "See here," he said, handing it to Ruby.

She took the fan, which was not the folding sort but a flat one on a stick, and carefully she turned it back and forth. Jesus in tinted pastels decorated one side, the rays of the sun behind him. On the other surface, in red ink on the gray-brown cardboard, a drawing of Bubba's store was centered above the stick.

"Cost seven cents apiece. Bought two hundred. So did Stevens. Hope it's hot enough tonight for people to use them."

"Praise the Lord," Ruby drew a deep breath. "Fourteen dollars is a lot of money these days."

"You're quick," said Bubba admiringly.

"I'm a manicurist. I don't have to count on my fingers. I count on others'."

"Shh! What brass!" A woman in front of them turned around to confront whoever was whispering during the opening hymn, and her eyes grew dark with surprise.

"Is that you, Ruby? Well, I never!"

"Good evening, Louise," said Bubba. "I see you know Ruby, too."

In Louise Haven's narrow blue eyes, Ruby saw breeding conquer curiosity. A town girl older than Ruby, Louise always seemed admirable, and she gained more stature as she forced a smile and a nod before swiveling back in her chair to face the pulpit.

"Yes," cried the preacher, "my text is First Corinthians: 'Now I see in the glass darkly, but then, face to face. And if I speak with the tongue of angels but have not love, I am as sounding brass.' Brass, ladies and gentlemen, brass, not gold, not silver, but ordinary brass. We *are* brass, we are base metal, we are corrupt. Corrupt as the rustiest tin can rotting on the dump, metal that base! We are sinners." The preacher unbuttoned his jacket.

It was warm in the tent. Ruby fluttered the fan with Bubba's store advertisement, and Jesus's face rose and fell before her. All around the tent, Jesus and Davidson's hovered in the air, and Bubba sat back in his chair, a smile playing about his full lips. He looked like someone who longed for a cigar.

"Love," shouted the preacher, and Bubba ceased slouching. Ruby too sat taller in her chair. "Love is the answer if you would not be brass." Bubba and Ruby gazed slyly at one another and grinned. She looked down. Bubba unhooked his thumb from his belt and let his hand rest on his thigh. Ruby lowered the fan and let it lie across her flowered skirt.

While the preacher spoke of the tongues of angels, she moistened her lips with the tip of her tongue.

"Praise the Lord!" the preacher continued. Louise Haven jumped up, bobbed her head, then sank into her seat.

"Amen," murmured a sea of faces around the island of Ruby and Bubba, who were now, under cover of the fan, wiggling their little fingers at one another.

"Rise, brothers! Rise, sisters!" exhorted the preacher, and the people rose up as one. Bubba and Ruby stood and slipped out of the tent, pausing only to step over an orange tabby kitten.

Bubba bent down, pulling his handkerchief from his pocket."Let me fix that," he said, and Ruby glanced to see what needed fixing. Her white leather pumps were stuck with bits of wet grass, for the field had been mown before the tent was assembled, and now the dew had set. They bumped heads, then laughed.

"Don't, Bubba," she said, pushing his hand away. "They'll only get grassy again. I'll clean them later." But she thought how sweet he was, and she could scarcely imagine that he, the owner of a store, provider of all those fans for the revival, would care enough for her, a girl from downriver, to clean her shoes. If he was so solicitous now, when they barely knew one another, what would he be like when they were lovers? Was it possible she would sleep with a Jew? He was very attractive, and although her mother would have a hissy fit if she were alive, somehow this only increased Ruby's interest. She steadied herself and studied his hands. He was busying himself with tucking his handkerchief back in his pocket and taking out a cigar.

He drove her home, surprised that she lived in the Camels' garage apartment. He himself lived only blocks away, he said. He was in Rotary with Ned Camel. He considered whether or not to kiss her goodnight. She could see him thinking of it.

"Bubba," she said, as they walked up the gravel to her door, "how 'bout we go fishing downriver come Sunday? I do believe I've had all the religion I need for awhile."

Then, standing on her stoop, she bent down and kissed him.

"A fine idea," he said, backing up, smiling broadly, and she couldn't tell whether he meant the kiss or the fishing. "I'll pick you up at seven o'clock; we'll get out there with the birds."

Ruby lay in bed that night considering the way his fingers laced through hers. She picked up Louise Haven's limp hand the next morning at the beauty parlor, thinking of the way he'd touched her. Louise came in every week, the same day, the same polite chitchat. Ruby thought today might be different.

"Quite a man," said Louise, speaking loudly from under the hair dryer.

Ruby nodded.

"Speaks with the tongue of angels himself," said Louise.

"You mean the preacher?"

"Who'd you think I meant? Oh, Bubba," Louise pursed her lips. "I didn't know you were seeing him," she said. "He's a regular rake and a gambling man. You be careful." Louise had been married for a couple of years and considered herself a matron. She remembered Ruby from high school, a tall country girl with hair a flaming cloud, whose voluptuous figure caused boys to turn and stare.

"You remember Booker Suggs?" Ruby asked.

"Booker? No, I don't," Louise said too quickly.

"Colored boy lived out our way, couldn't ride the bus to school, and the colored school another mile past the high school? You don't remember the fuss? I asked the driver to let him on one day, it was raining so hard."

"I think I recall it now, but I wasn't on the bus. I only heard of it," said Louise faintly.

"Driver called me a nigger-lover," said Ruby. "I told him he was no Christian and no gentleman. He reported me. Everyone called me nigger-lover that year, my first year of high school."

"Now I remember," said Louise, and she stared at her hand as Ruby bent to paint the undercoat carefully on her nails. Her hand looked small and powerless, unlike Ruby's.

"The thing is," said Ruby, laying Louise's hand to one side of the table, taking the other from the soapy water and toweling it dry, "since then I learned it don't matter much what people say. I do as I please, so long as it don't hurt anybody."

"He's Jewish," said Louise. "The Davidson boys grew up with me. They're real nice mannered and not pushy. They're very smart. Still, it's just as well we don't have many in this town. I hear they band together when there's a lot of them. They mostly marry their own, too. You would *never* fit in; excuse me for saying so." Louise rattled on. "I play bridge with Maude, Doc's wife. Doc is Bubba's older brother. She's a real lady, a lot older than we are, but she knows her own mind. I don't know what she'd make of you—hash probably, if you let her. Ouch," she squealed, "that orange stick went to the quick."

Ruby didn't apologize. Louise went on. "Bubba's waited too long to marry. You be careful. How old are you, anyway?"

"Old enough," said Ruby, "to go fishing with him on Sunday." She studied her own hands for a moment. "I think I'll do my nails when I finish yours. I want to look nice for him, even if it's only fishing."

She did. She wore a brown-and-yellow-checked sundress starched and ironed, and brown fishing shoes, no nonsense, and a straw hat, mostly for effect. She'd made sandwiches and a thermos of coffee, and she was waiting by the window behind the curtain when he drove up in his green Hudson a few minutes before the hour. Happy to see him, she noticed his straw hat, his clean-shaven chin, all with approval. "I brought the best bait," he said, "chicken innards." Ruby shook her head agreeably although she preferred dead minnows herself. Bait was a matter of belief, as peculiar as religion.

Later that day, about noon, with catfish in a tin bucket anchored at the river's edge, they sat finishing her sandwiches and drinking beer he'd brought. Ruby fanned away mosquitoes with one of the revival fans Bubba had taken.

"What did you think of that revival?"

"I enjoyed the company," he said. "Being Jewish, I can't say I followed the text. Of course, I *do* believe in love, but I am not in the business of scrap iron. All that talk."

"You mean you don't know Corinthians?"

"New Testament. I'm afraid not."

"Do you think you'll go to hell?"

"Do you?"

She threw back her head and laughed. "Well, I never. I don't believe I've ever had such a conversation. Do I think you'll go to hell?" She set down her beer can and clasped her arms around her knees. "I like it that you take me serious."

"I believe hell is here on earth," she continued cautiously. She looked at Bubba to see how he took this heresy, but he merely looked interested. "I think it's going on in Europe now. My brother's over there, and I read the newspapers. I see the newsreels in the picture show." She bit her lip. "Also," she said, "I've heard terrible things about those POWs over to Fort Robinson."

"You been over there? What call you have to go there?"

"My sister, Martha Nell, works for the Red Cross in Little Rock. I was visiting with her one day when they had to deliver packages. She was too scared to go alone. It was silly, no call to be worried. There's guards and lots of protection. You don't really get near the prisoners. Funny, though, they've learned English, some of them, and they want to talk, they call to you, but the guards don't let them. We gave them a good looking over, I can tell you," she said mischievously.

"I've heard they're killing Jews in Europe," Bubba replied, "people like me. Doesn't matter that they haven't done anything wrong, except they're Jewish. I can't believe it. It doesn't seem possible, but if it's true, then I believe in hell right here too."

Together they sat quietly, chewing on stalks of grass, watching the muddy river throw off glints of light in the Arkansas noon. Dragonflies flitted over a half-submerged log. Floating past on old rubber inner tubes, two boys kicked and splashed one another, hooting at Bubba and Ruby from the river. Minutes passed, and Ruby thought how strange the conversation had been, considering how peaceful she felt just now, how safe and apart from whatever was happening over there. To be speaking of hell like that excited her. Lord, she hoped there wasn't a hell. She felt shivery happy. She picked up the fan again and took a good look at Jesus.

"I don't know for sure," said Bubba, "but I believe I am as happy as I've ever been right this very moment." He lay back against the hickory tree and crossed his arms across his chest, his fishing pole propped up in case anything bit.

He broke off another stalk of timothy and began to chew on it, squinting at Ruby.

"You say that to all your girls?" Louise's caution blew in her ears like a chill wind.

"Happiness is nothing to make light of," he said, sitting upright. He took the fan from her and smoothed her hair. She moved closer to him, gentled. Bubba flipped the fan from one side to the other. "You can put faith or its symbol on this fan." He poked at the drawing of his store. "But you tell me, can you put real happiness on the back of a fan? You can't draw it," he said, "only if you have it; when you haven't had it, then you know it unless you're a damn fool." He chucked the tip of the fan under her chin.

Ruby took the fan and set it down with Jesus's face smiling into the matted grass, Davidson's store face up. She saw then how her life could be. She was glad of it, something she had never known, that she could be the cause of someone's happiness, and she realized that she too was happy. She shivered, delighted to be wanted—she didn't doubt he wanted her—to be *needed*—she didn't doubt he needed her. Nobody had ever spoken to her of happiness. Mostly boys had pawed at her and gasped over her, taking, only taking. Bubba was giving, and desire for him surprised her just as a fish hit on his line.

"Look there!" he cried as the pole dipped deep into the river, and she rolled over to clear his path toward the pole, but he rolled after her and murmured into her hair, "Let that one get away, but not this." Ruby turned to say yes and she felt his back damp with perspiration, his shirt soft against her. Carefully she lifted one lacquered finger to his temple, just to smooth the place where there would be a horn if one believed in such things. Then she kissed him full on the mouth, letting her hand fall away.

Butterflies

"I don't know," said Martha Nell. "You knew when you married him he was older. You must've known John Clay would come back from the war. Or did you think he'd die over there and save you the trouble of telling him?"

Ruby walked over to the tea cart that held Bubba's liquor. She poured herself a shot of bourbon neat and didn't say anything until she'd drunk it. Then, refilling the glass again, she shrugged her shoulders. "I'm free, white, and over twenty-one," she told her sister.

"Twenty," Martha Nell interrupted, "and married."

Ruby was irritable. "It was just fine, you know, until John Clay came home. He came to the shop looking for me, and Gladys told him I wasn't doing manicures. She told him I was working with Bubba."

"He never got your letters?"

"Never did."

"And so?" Martha Nell bit off a piece of gold yarn and looked up from her needlework, her green eyes reminding Ruby of a cat stalking a bird. She wound the thread around her finger without ever taking her eyes off Ruby.

"He walked right into the store, back where I was marking stock, straightaway looks hard at Bubba over by the hosiery counter where he's waiting on a customer, and says, big as you please, 'What in the Sam Hill has been goin' on?'

"Bubba hears his voice, not what he said, but something about the manner of his saying it, and *he* looks over, wondering.

"'Hush,' I told John Clay. I wanted to hug and kiss him, not having seen him for three years, but I let my hands stay where they were, full of pins and cardboard. My stomach was full of butterflies. 'So you're back,' was all I said. He had on blue jeans and a plaid shirt, boots, and a straw hat. His pants were tight, you could see every little rise, and it was rising, let me tell you. He'd shaved his hair. You recall how dark and thick it was? It's cut close; it makes his features sharp, and his eyes, you remember how I used say they fairly burned right through me? They're still the same, looking right into my soul.

He can still get to me. I backed away a little, practically into the Coke machine there at the back next to Layaway.

"This raised Bubba's suspicion. He called over to me: was everything all right, did I need any help, sugar? It was the "sugar" that did it. John Clay looks straightaway to my hand, he sees the ring"... now Ruby held out her left hand, studied the small diamond set in gold, let it fall into her lap, and continued. "'My God,' he says, 'I don't believe it.' He looks hard at me, and harder still at Bubba. 'He's *old*,' he says. 'Whatever can you be thinkin' of?' And then he turns and stumbles up the aisle out of the store."

Martha Nell was bent over her embroidery now, squinting but listening carefully.

"Of course Bubba wanted to know what it was all about. I told him before I married him I had been keeping company with John Clay, only it wasn't serious." Ruby looked up over her empty glass, her red hair falling into her shoulders as if it were heavily weighted. "It never was, for me. It was mostly hustle and tussle, far as I'm concerned. It's been finished with since I met Bubba." Ruby shrugged.

She had been married for over a year now, although it seemed like yesterday that Bubba had hurried her off to a justice of the peace in Wynne, afraid that his family would raise objections unless he and Ruby presented themselves already beyond the reach of their entreaties. He'd used a French expression, she hardly knew where he got it, a *fait accompli*, he'd called it. She had asked him if *accompli* meant worse than death, because if that was what he meant, she didn't plan to marry him.

He had laughed, and said that she tickled him, that it gave him pleasure to think of spending the rest of his life with her, his baby, his sugar, his sweet.

That was how Ruby felt too. She'd been very happy until yesterday when John Clay showed up, mustered out of the army, ready to take up where he'd left off. She leaned back in her chair, playing her fingers over the hobnails, thinking how it used to be with them. She sighed. Martha Nell was echoing her words.

"Hustle and tussle, that's some name for it. You *are* a mess, a regular mess. Maybe worse than me."

Ruby sat up straight. "Do not judge lest ye be judged," she said sharply. "*I* never got myself p.g., Martha Nell. You are a fine one to talk."

But now, while Martha Nell began to backtrack and apologize, Ruby sat there barely listening, wondering how and why it was that she wasn't pregnant now. Bubba was eager for a family and so was she, but nothing had happened that way. She felt Miss Sissie's eyes on her when they went over to his mother's for Sunday dinners, but her abdomen remained disappointingly flat. One of Maude's and Doc's daughters had just had a baby. Ruby wanted one too, found herself praying every month out of disappointment and longing.

Women came into the store to buy oversized dresses, cotton shifts. She knew they were pregnant, and she envied them. Doris Jean, her old friend from high school, had quit her job at the restaurant to marry Danny Harrels in a hurry. A year from now, people would forget they'd had to get married, and Doris Jean would be pushing a perambulator up and down the uneven sidewalk like the other young women. Ruby sighed.

"Guess I've worn out my welcome," Martha Nell was saying. "'Pears to me you haven't heard a word I've said." She was standing now and putting away her sewing.

"I've got a lot on my mind," Ruby said, but she didn't encourage her sister to stay. Bubba would be coming home soon, and between remembering John Clay and thinking of a baby, she wanted to be alone.

But later, lying on their bed, smelling his cigar, listening to the radio, feeling the evening creep into the house, purple and blue over the rose of Sharon outside their bedroom window, Ruby was surprised by sadness. She rolled over on one elbow and gazed at Bubba. His eyes were closed, but his teeth clenched the cigar, and he was not asleep. He opened his eyes and saw her there, the hand-painted bedside lamp behind her like a rosy halo.

He pushed himself up and placed his cigar in the ashtray on his nightstand. "Looks like you lost your best friend."

"I'm not pregnant, Bubba. It's been over a year."

He pulled her down and rested her head on his shoulder. The thin strap of his tee shirt rubbed against her cheek, but she lay still while he stroked her hair.

"You don't want to see Doc about it, I'll drive you over to Memphis," he said. "Take you to a doctor there. That suit you?"

"Who will mind the store?"

"Don't worry about that."

They drove the next week to a clinic specializing in female problems, but after a series of tests, it was determined that nothing was the matter with Ruby. Driving back to Arkansas in the green Hudson, Bubba smoked his cigar and frowned. He pulled his fedora down to avoid the glare from the setting sun. Ruby could barely see his face between the hat and the smoke.

"I don't know," he muttered, "I just don't know what to make of it."

"What do you mean?"

"The idea," said Bubba, "that having mumps might be the problem. It was bad enough to have mumps. Everyone teased me. Maude's kids had 'em and I caught 'em too. But that's—lemme think— three, four years ago. What took my attention wasn't the mumps; it was not getting into the army. I'd volunteered but they found some heart flutter from when I was a kid and had rheumatic fever. That *really* upset me, everyone volunteering and me having to stay home. I never thought nothin' about those mumps." He pushed his hat up and flipped the gray visor down on the car. He pulled off the road onto a spit of pink and orange gravel and threw the stub of his cigar back onto the road. Ruby turned to look at him but over his shoulder she could see the tiny bit of tobacco smolder on the asphalt, and she watched it as if her life depended on it until its glow turned to ash.

"Well, now," she started, unable to think of anything else to say. After the doctor had examined her, he had called Bubba into his office while she sat idly leafing through magazines in the waiting room. "Nothing wrong with her" hummed in her ears while she sat there, beat against her like the wings of a hummingbird. Her whole being sang with the pleasure of nothing wrong with her, and the world looked fresh, even the doctor's waiting room with the brass humidor filled with dirty sand and cigarette butts. Less than an hour had passed since then. Stunned now, Ruby continued to stare at the dead cigar ash in the road. At length she turned to look him, his face twice gray with anguish and stubble. There were tears in his eyes.

Along the roadside sprawled trumpet vines whose orange flowers gave her something to look at other than the gray. Intuitively she focused on the vine, the way it climbed out of the dusty ditch and hugged the barbed wire effortlessly, the way it sought the light, also, as it was late in the afternoon, the way the blossoms closed protectively until next day.

"Sweetheart, Bubba, honey. This is not the end of the world. This is just a man in a white coat saying *maybe* the mumps could be a problem." She covered his face in kisses until its pallor flowered with bright red lipstick, and then she took out her handkerchief, spit on it, and tried to wipe it off. "You are a mess," she said. "You look like a regular circus clown."

"But what if he's right?" Bubba could barely manage the words.

"Well, then I'll be your baby, and you will just be mine." He hugged her close, and over his head she stared at the trumpet vine until her own eyes cleared and were dry again. Please, she prayed, please, God.

The next day, back at the store, she spent the morning reviewing sales slips from the day before when they had been in Memphis. Louise Haven had come in and bought a cotton dress, size 12. Ruby knew what that meant. Still, she tallied everything carefully before she and Bubba went home for dinner at noon. After their meal, she lay down with a headache, and Bubba told her to stay put. He didn't need her at the store except on weekends. Ruby lay on the bed feeling the crocheted bedspread rasp against her calves. She stared for awhile at a picture on the wall next to her maple dresser. Bubba didn't know it, but John Clay had sent her that picture as a souvenir from the South Seas when he had first been sent over there.

Made from the wings of butterflies, all silvery blue and orange and black, the picture was of a boat sailing over the water, but you couldn't see where it was going. She thought her life might turn out like that, uncertain of direction but essentially colorful. She wondered how many dead butterflies it took to make the picture, and she wondered too who killed them, who fashioned the picture, what life was like in that place. She was sure, lying there, that it must have been a question of survival. She imagined a Philippine woman sitting in a grass skirt making the picture of the boat. Ruby's head ached. She took an aspirin and slept. She woke dry-mouthed, breathless, anxious.

She decided to walk Uptown to the A&P to buy a small piece of ham and black-eyed peas for tomorrow. The peas had to soak overnight. She applied her makeup and dressed for her walk as if she was going to Maude's for a Coke. She might, she thought, stop off there on her way back from the grocery. But at the A&P, who did she run into in the parking lot but John Clay himself, and because she didn't want to be seen standing and talking to him there where everyone was running into the store for last minute tomatoes and okra and cornmeal, she found herself agreeing to a lift home.

"Before I take you home, let's drive out to the orchards," said John Clay. "I promised my mama I'd pick up a bushel of peaches. She's canning. You can tell me all about it," he said, both hands tight on the steering wheel. He looked straight down the highway, gripping a toothpick between his teeth. He smelled of sweat and starch and danger, like always.

"I have to get back," she said faintly. "I have to cook supper. Bubba comes home at 5:30."

John Clay just looked at her out of the corner of his eye, allowing his toothpick to droop over his lip.

The edge of town blurred past, a few houses built on stilts, a series of empty lots, and then a vast openness that spoke of cotton and soybeans, hard impoverished soil and despair. There was a small shack shingled with yellow asbestos siding, colored children on the porch and under it, barely clothed, their eyes vacant as they stared at John Clay's car. It wasn't any different from any other car that passed this way, a man staring straight ahead, a woman turning aside. They had, she thought, no sense of themselves as scenery. They were people, real children, so many of them for one house, no mother in sight, only a girl about fourteen, in a pink and brown dress, staring back as Ruby stared at her, without curiosity or enthusiasm.

"Children so cute," said Ruby, but John Clay didn't answer. He remained silent all the way to the edge of the peach orchard, where he drove the car not up to the scales and the crates of fruit, but down a long side-aisle through the peach trees, coming to a halt in the dust and weeds at the far end of the orchard. The tree nearest them was old, and Ruby fixed her eyes on a blob of amber sap that ran from a gash in a limb bent down toward the hood of John Clay's car.

"That sap'll make a fine mess if it gets on your car," she said. She wasn't nervous except that she felt a physical stirring, the kind he always aroused in her. She had hoped now she was married that this shimmery feeling had disappeared, dried up and fallen away except with respect to Bubba, but here it was in spite of what she hoped. Her skin felt transparent, and she could tell, as he turned to reproach her in the middle of the fruit orchard, that he could *feel* her desire. She concentrated on the peach sap, globules that clustered along the trunk to no purpose. She scratched her arm absently.

"Fine mess," John Clay said, "don't talk to *me* about fine messes. How come you married him? Wasn't I good enough?" Roughly he took her hand and scrutinized the diamond Bubba had given her. "You never cared about fancy stuff with me," he said.

"Don't. You don't know *what* I cared about. We never had any understanding between us, except . . ." Ruby hesitated to describe the way they had of giving pleasure without words.

But as if her unaccustomed reticence had recalled their former passion, John Clay now reached for her and pulled her to him, crushing her into the front seat, where the plastic knob of the window handle pressed the top of her head as she lay pinned beneath him.

She asked herself later why she hadn't resisted him, how much responsibility she had. When she reconstructed the afternoon, which she could do by simply standing still and closing her eyes, or by walking into her kitchen and picking up a fuzzy peach from the pressed glass bowl on her white enamel table, Ruby had always to come back to the fact that her hips tilted to his as hungrily as ever they had before her marriage.

"Only this once," she told him, and John Clay laughed.

"Girl, who you kidding?"

For two weeks she tormented herself with that afternoon, sometimes telling herself that it had only happened because she was upset over the man she now called the mumps doctor. John Clay had taken advantage of her, trading on the irresistible physical attraction they had always felt for one another.

Ruby doubled her efforts at housekeeping, polishing silver, shining brass, dusting furniture. She took to visiting her sister-in-law Maude in the mornings, buffered by the presence of Maude's daughter and grandchildren who were visiting from

St. Louis. Maude and Doc kept a decanter of bourbon on the sideboard in her dining room, and Ruby
splashed a little into her Coke when she refilled
the glasses for everyone during those visits. She
made up a manicure kit for Maude's grandchildren
and painted their toes and fingernails, marveling
at their tiny fingers. She was so occupied with the
children, basking in their evident admiration, that
almost a week passed before Ruby noticed that she
had missed a period.

She walked around praying for another week,
but nothing happened. She tried to tell Bubba, but
his dark mood prevented her. More preoccupied
than she had ever seen him, he was almost beyond
reach in some sorrowful place. Finally she brought
herself to corner Doc one afternoon when she and
Bubba had stayed for the noon meal. Maude didn't
like the smell of Doc's Dutch Masters cigars, and he
smoked them after lunch on the side porch. If a Cardinals game was being broadcast from St. Louis, he
would string the cord beneath the screen door and
set the radio down on the porch beside him.

"Doc," said Ruby, smoothing her skirt, sitting
down in a wicker rocker opposite him, raising her
voice above Harry Caray and the Cardinals, but
keeping it low enough to prevent being overheard,

"I think I'm pregnant. I'm two weeks late. I haven't told Bubba yet."

"Well, don't," said Doc abruptly. "You're not pregnant. Dr. Blander explained to Bubba about the mumps. I've been explaining it all over again this week. You know what that means, don't you? You're just upset about it, and you have a right to be. Being upset can make you miss a time. I'm sorry, Ruby, but you and Bubba cannot have children together."

"Absolutely?"

"Positively."

Then what, she wondered, and why? She imagined all the eggs she had been born with clustered inside her like the tray of grapes held by the smiling young woman on the raisin box. Lord, how she wanted a baby, but as the month wore on, she became nervous. Doc always knew what he was talking about. And if she couldn't have a child with Bubba, then what was this?

Ruby lay on her bed most afternoons, feeling faint, staring at the picture made from crushed butterflies. She held imaginary conversations with the woman in the Philippines who had made the picture. What should I do? she asked. You do what you must to survive, said the distant woman. You try to make it as beautiful as you can, said the woman, and sometimes you even put a frame around it. You call it your life.

Ruby told Bubba she was going shopping in Memphis with Martha Nell and went to see Dr. Blander again, telling her sister that it was a follow-up visit. Martha Nell sat in the waiting room doing needlepoint while Ruby saw the doctor.

"I don't understand this," he said. "It's physically impossible for your husband to father a child, and yet here you are pregnant. Well, congratulations are in order." He looked narrowly at her as she began to cry. "Or are they?"

Ruby's eyes ran. "I cannot have this baby," she said finally. "It was an accident. Almost a rape, you could say."

"There's no such thing as a little bit pregnant," said the doctor. "Almost a rape? Either it was or it wasn't."

"I knew the man," she said in a low voice. "I love my husband. I cannot have this baby."

"Do you love him enough for that?" She stared down at her perfect nails, looked at the ring Bubba had given her, thought of the way he had looked on the highway back from Memphis, drawn and gray and anguished. She imagined herself sitting on a cushion patiently sifting color from the wings of butterflies while the woman from the raisin box stood waiting for her to put down the butterflies and take a grape. But she never looked up. No, she seemed to whisper, those are not for me.

She looked up again at the doctor. She sniffed, then slipped her hand into her purse and felt for her compact. She took it out and powdered her red nose, then slid it back into her purse while the doctor sat there looking pained. She rose and gazed out the window over low rooftops and used car lots. The shimmer of hot metal shot shards of cutting light in the summer sun. She could feel his eyes on her back, and she stood straight and tall.

"Women know about these things. Where to go. But it *is* dangerous. You could die of it, and I don't want to die. I have a good life with Bubba. It will have to be enough."

Then she sat back down. "Dr. Blander, you went to medical school with Doc. This has to be very private, just between you and me." When Ruby left the office, pale and shaken, she was no longer pregnant.

"You look awful," said Martha Nell cheerfully, winding up her embroidery. "Are you going to have a baby?"

"No," said Ruby, "I'm not."

"There's always hope. These doctors don't know everything. You can always pray for a miracle, you know. Sometimes a person's prayers are answered when they least expect it." She took her brass thimble and popped it into her sewing bag.

Ruby bit her lip. She opened her purse and took out some Dentyne gum. She had a bad taste in her mouth.

"Oh, Martha Nell," she said, slipping the gum back into her purse only to discover that her compact had sprung open, dusting everything with face powder. "I am going to be careful the way I pray for the rest of my life," she said. She withdrew her powdery fingers and rubbed them together over the brass humidor in the doctor's waiting room.

"I'm going to be very careful. Or maybe I won't pray at all. There's lots of ways to get through life, Martha Nell."

Ruby's Gift

Ruby, who was married to Mother's Uncle Bubba, stood five foot ten inches in her stocking feet, with masses of red hair and a pompadour that increased her stature to six feet when she sucked in her stomach, squared her shoulders, and leveled her chin at the world. Her world was a small one, but it had all the ingredients needed for love and glory and backbiting and the like. Bubba, the youngest of the great-uncles, owned a store Uptown. We didn't call it Downtown. This small town in Arkansas which we visited each summer had no Downtown. There was Uptown, Colored Town, and the rest of town, which stopped someplace near the cemetery at the edge of town. Everything beyond that was called country or downriver.

Ruby came from downriver. She wasn't country. We didn't know exactly what she was, but she fascinated us. As we were only summer visitors, we never got to see her in her coat with the fox collar. Indeed, after the afternoon of the scandalous behavior, I was rarely to see her again for a long time, but the fact that Ruby owned such a coat, with little beady eyes staring out from where it hung in the cedar closet, the mere fact of ownership put her up a notch in our estimation. We had never been downriver ourselves. We thought, however, that it must be a dark and mysterious place, filled with peril and catfish, like the ditch that ran along the edge of our grandmother's property.

Since it was off-limits, the ditch and the surrounding ravine held terror for us, and consequently drew us, each morning after breakfast, to its edge. A double rail of black and rusted iron had been driven into the sidewalk to keep people from falling in. We were doubtless the people the managers of the telephone company had in mind when they drove the rail. They owned the ditch, and they owned the rail, but we owned the time. Every morning my cousin Elizabeth and I would settle ourselves on the rim of the sidewalk, stick our bare feet underneath the railing, and pitch bits of cement from where the concrete crumbled down into the opaque brown water in hopes of making a fish jump or rousing a snake.

One morning, to our great satisfaction, we were successful. The pebble-rippled ditch lay some thirty feet beneath our outstretched toes, and out of its surface slithered a king snake, over a log and through the dense green leaves up toward Miz Lillian's backyard. We went screaming over there, knocking breathlessly on the back door until the maid, Hattie, came around to see what was the matter.

"Snake, snake," we shouted, "coming out of the ditch into the yard, Hattie!" Against all odds, sure enough, when Hattie had fetched Walter, Miz Lillian's twelve-year-old son, and when Walter had whistled next door for Joe Boy, our fourteen-year-old uncle, and when we all marched back of the garden to investigate, there was the snake, lying as big as you please, next to the circular flower bed that was the centerpiece of Lillian's garden. The bed held zinnias the size of your hand, salvia, and blue ageratum ordered direct from the Burpee catalogue. The snake lay near the flowers, sunning, resting after its exit from the ditch.

Walter and Joe Boy took down an ax from Mr. Danforth's garage. They cut the arrogant snake in two and then in three, and part of it wiggled and jerked in the grass though severed from its head until finally it went limp while we watched, fascinated by its demise. The grass had gone dry beneath our toes as the sun got hotter. Our throats were dry too, and suddenly anxious now that the deed was done, we wished that our mothers would come out of the front room where they sat behind venetian blinds and tried to stay cool, sipping Coca-Colas with our grandmother.

"We've killed us a fine big snake," we bragged, dancing barefoot on the carpet. "Come and see, Grandmother! Come and see, everyone."

"Ladies do not kill snakes," Grandmother said.

"Really Joe Boy and Walter killed it," we confessed by way of appeasement, but we felt as if we had killed it ourselves. "Please come," we entreated, but our mothers took their cue from Grandmother and declined the honor, saying they'd see it another time. Only Ruby, paying a morning visit, came out into the garden to inspect what was left of the snake.

"When might there *be* another time?" she asked the privet hedge. "Boy, you done slithered your last," she said with some satisfaction, and she smiled down at the bits of snake drying out in the sun. "That's one snake I don't have to be looking after when next I go downriver for my catfish," and she cracked her Dentyne gum two or three times.

"Jus' one thing," she added soberly. "That snake's no poisonous snake, y'all know that?"

"Snakes the incarnation of evil," said Hattie.

"Sure enough right about that, Hattie," Ruby replied, "but some snakes are different from others, and it helps to know what kind of snake you be dealing with."

We all stood around there in the Danforths' back garden, my cousin and I, Joe Boy and Walter, and Hattie and Ruby, reflecting on snakes, secretly wishing then that the snake had been a copperhead or a cottonmouth. Then Hattie ventured, "You be looking fine, Miz Ruby."

"This here's Rita Hayworth red," said Ruby, tossing her long hair about her white shoulders. "Rita Hayworth red, Hattie," and she reknotted the tie to her midriff as we all stood there admiring her ample curves and her flaming red hair and her high-heeled shoes that looked like snakeskin, especially like the part of the snake that was bloody. Ruby bent down to scratch a chigger on her ankle, and her shoulders came into our line of vision. They were white and smooth, but they had *freckles* at the edges. They were, so far as we knew, the only freckles on an adult white female in the whole of that small Arkansas town, Uptown and the rest of town included. It was a revelation.

Then, taking the full measure of our devotion, Ruby moved with dignity back through the parting in the hedge where we had worn a path, and she stepped high through the tall grass where the yard-man had failed to mow close to the hedge. Walter whistled a low whistle, half to himself, and Hattie rapped him one on the head.

"Hush your sass and be respectful," she said severely, and waving toward the garage, she directed him to clean his father's ax and put it away.

"Fine figure of a woman," said Hattie to the ageratum before she marched herself back to Miz Lillian's kitchen.

We loved Ruby for coming into the garden to see the dead snake. We admired her for going down-river with Bubba to fish. Our mothers, though only a few years younger than Ruby, were Grandmother's daughters to the core. They walked my cousin and me Uptown for paper dolls and lime Cokes some afternoons, but they never went fishing. They didn't crack their gum, and they didn't have about them the scent of adventure Ruby exuded like the heavy perfume she favored that came in a midnight blue bottle brought by Bubba from Memphis.

With her freckles and heady perfume, her long red nails and her fox-collared coat, Ruby was something. One of a kind, Grandmother declared, as if it was a curse. Grandfather spoke as if making a diagnosis: unique, he said. Though Bubba was his younger brother, Grandfather spoke at times as though he were his son instead.

"Bubba," he said, "that young wife of yours is the only woman I know who's a good bluff in a poker game." Bubba looked faintly embarrassed.

"Doc," he said, "I'm crazy about that damn fool woman, don't care who knows it. I just wish Maude liked her more."

"Maude's Maude, and Ruby's Ruby. Ruby's damn near young enough to be our daughter, Bubba."

Cheerfully Bubba agreed, but then he added, "There's more to it than age, Doc. You were right the first time. Maude's Maude, and Ruby's Ruby."

Grandfather grunted deep in his throat, and then he said something that mystified us further. "Only," he said, "she drinks too much for her own damn good."

That started us watching, Elizabeth and I, the next time that Ruby came to call. We sat with our paper dolls on the floor while the grownups visited, and we watched from the corners of our eyes. Ruby did not appear to drink more than our mothers or Grandmother. In fact, when the time came for refilling the glasses, Ruby volunteered, as she usually did, to go back to the pantry to pour out the second round. Following along, we observed that she was generous to a fault. First, she was long on soda and short on ice, just the opposite of Grandmother. Furthermore, she asked us did we want to share, and then she splashed the soda out of her glass and into our juice glasses, making up the difference in her own half-empty one with the Jack Daniel's whiskey that stood in the decanter on the sideboard. Ruby made certain that everyone else had plenty of Coke and only shortchanged herself.

And Ruby was generous with her catfish, too. Our big meal of the day when we visited in Arkansas was dinner, and it was served at noon. But on the Sunday evenings of the catfish days of Ruby and Bubba, then Lena stayed late to help with the fish fry that always followed their return. Bubba and Ruby would come driving around to the back door dripping catfish, they'd say of themselves, like a couple of backwoodsmen. Lena and Bubba and Ruby, too, with her long red fingernails, would cut the heads off the fish and gut and clean them there on the porch over a wide tin bucket.

Ruby was as handy with the ice pick as she was with the knife.

"Let me do that, Lena," she'd say. She'd take Lena's ice pick, and while Lena stood there wiping her large brown hands on her broad white apron, Ruby chipped at the block of ice with an energy that was alarming. Over the hum of the Frigidaire and over the tapping of Lena's foot, we could hear Ruby mutter as she chipped, "an' that for you, Miz Hampton, and that for you, you sonovabitch John Clay Ferris." When we ventured to ask her "What's that you say, Ruby?" she laughed a sobbing kind of laugh and said "Never you mind, darlings." Then she chipped meticulously but silently until all the ice was whittled away into the tub that held the catfish.

Then, as if rage could be whittled like ice, Ruby smiled and whispered as though imparting a secret, "Milk first, then the cornmeal, Lena." Lena nodded and said in a soothing voice like honey for a sore throat, "They'll crisp up real fine, Miz Ruby. They's good fish."

Ruby winked a broad wink, hitched her brassiere into alignment, and chuckled at some unspoken joke between them. "These catfish come real easy downriver, like one-two-three downriver. And I thank you, Lena, for missin' your Sunday night meeting on account of these damned fish," she added formally. Then Lena, repeating her part of the ritual, nodded graciously and said that she didn't mind, because Mr. Bubba and Miz Ruby didn't go downriver every Sunday but only once in a while.

"An' I know you work real hard up to the store with Mr. Bubba on Saturdays," she added charitably. No one else acknowledged that Ruby worked at all, let alone hard, and what Lena said seemed to please her enormously.

"Credit," she laughed with a short bark, "where credit is due."

Grandmother sat at one end of the long dinner table, took a silver serving piece that was broad and flat, and slid the fried fish onto the silver, then onto the plates before her, deliberately, as if she was weighing each crisp catfish.

"I must give you credit, Bubba, for a very fine catch."

So predictable was her pronouncement that on one occasion we saw Bubba wink at Ruby even as Grandmother spoke.

"Credit where credit is due" was painted with black ink and stencil from Woolworth's, then hung on a piece of tattered cardboard at the back of Bubba's store, over the Coke machine. Elizabeth and I were free to walk Uptown almost any afternoon, but we tried to arrange our visits to the store to coincide with Ruby's Saturdays. We would find her standing behind the front counter in carpet slippers, making sales in ladies' finery.

"My, they look real, do they not?" she exclaimed, clapping her hands in genuine admiration at a navy straw hat with fake cherries on the brim. Her hands flashed, and her long red fingernails plucked at the cherries. The tired old farm woman across the counter squinted at the hat, then gingerly placed it on her head over the rags that tied her hair in place. The two women peered together into the mirror that stood on the counter's edge, and the old woman murmured almost to herself, "Yes'm, they sure do look real. Wonder do those blackbirds chase me if'n I wear this hat to church?" Then both Ruby and the woman laughed at the joke, and they came to a low-voiced agreement about the price, which Ruby always knocked a dollar from, as if Bubba knew nothing about such things.

In the nether parts of the store, behind the Coke machine, under a no-nonsense sign that said "Layaway," there hung a gown, the most beautiful I had ever seen. It had first been in the front window of the store, on a mannequin, shielded from the glare by a strip of yellow plastic stretched across the glass. While it was there, my cousin and I would linger at the display, and when no one was looking, finger the stiff black tulle that stuck out in billows from the tiny waist. The pink satin bodice was strapless, shirred, and sequined. It even had rosebuds on it. Now that the gown was back in Layaway under the credit sign, the sequins glittered and winked at us from the dark alcove. The tulle had been cased in a cleaner's bag for safekeeping; we could no longer touch it.

Every Saturday afternoon, a young woman came into the store to put down money on the dress. Gravely Ruby would withdraw a book for recording the transaction from her shelf under the counter, and she'd scratch off some numbers. The woman would mark an X next to where Ruby had figured. Too young to compute, I asked, "Will Lizzie get the dress to take home with her before I go back to St. Louis in August?"

"No, sugar," Ruby said, "Lizzie be lucky to get that dress while she still be slim enough to wear it. Lizzie be payin' on that dress for a long time, sugar." She shook her head sadly, and she pursed her lips as if she disapproved mightily of something. Then she shrugged, put her hand under the counter, and pulled out some Dentyne gum to share with us.

When Elizabeth and I had stayed out of the forbidden ditch for days at a time, when we'd refrained from picking at scabs and from being "uppity," then we were allowed the privilege of staying the night with Ruby and Bubba, who had no children of their own. After they had feted us as only childless couples can, after we'd peeked into the cedar closet to see the fox faces on her coat, after Ruby had taken out her special manicuring tray and painted our fingers and toes, we were tucked into bed in satin comforters, in cool sheets that smelled of almonds, and we stared until we fell asleep at the painted lamps with roses on milk glass. There were brass keys for turning up the wicks, although actually the lamps were electrified, much like Ruby herself, and they gave off, as she did, a rosy glow.

Ruby always said as she tucked us in for the night, that if we were good, then we could have lamps like that too when we grew up. She had made the same sure prediction about satin gowns as well, and it was a source of great satisfaction to believe that such were the earthly rewards for being good and growing up.

"Foolishness," said Grandmother when we repeated that we would have pink satin gowns when we grew up. "Nonsense," said our elders when we admired the rose lamps. But they said more than that on the afternoon of the scandalous behavior. They said more and then they said nothing, and Ruby was consigned to memory, for after that day, we didn't see her again for a very long time.

We were gathered for the noonday meal. Ruby had spent the morning drinking Coca-Colas with the women. Bubba had worked at the store. Lena had set the table for a southern feast. Fried chicken was heaped on platters, yams swam in syrup in a tureen, turnip greens steamed from matched bowls at either end of the table, and the gravy boat on its stand was already dripping over the edge. Everything was in place, including attitudes. The children were sequestered at the end of the table; the main conversation occurred at Grandfather's end. Our job was to keep quiet, clean our plates, and chew with our mouths closed. But our mouths dropped open when Ruby talked back to Grandmother, breaking the unspoken rule that no one crossed the hostess at her own table.

Bubba and Grandfather had come in with the noon whistle, straight from the clinic and the store. Bubba was telling a story about a man who had come into the store to buy on credit. Grandfather, the country doctor who got paid in bushel baskets of green beans or okra when he got paid at all, had a certain sympathy for the man in Bubba's store. Grandmother did not.

"Nigger rich," she snorted, "paid on Friday, spent on Saturday." She spat the words out with a vehemence that made everyone look up. It did not seem likely that she was speaking only of the customer, whoever he was.

We shot glances at one another, and so it was that we saw Ruby calmly put down her fork and pat her lips with her large linen napkin the way a person does when the meal is over.

"And why not?" she asked. She continued defiantly, ignoring Bubba's pained expression, squaring her shoulders in the direction of Grandmother's wide eyes and flaring nostrils.

"Why indeed not? How come y'all so sure you'll live to see tomorrow? Live for today. Tomorrow comes, there's time enough to worry about it. Nigger rich," she snorted, "you don't know what rich is. You, Maude: poorest excuse of all—you criticize them for living today when they not sure about tomorrow? Dumbest nigger in this town got more sense than you, weighing your catfish, measuring your damned ice cubes into a glass, measuring everything that melts away. I can't hardly stand it."

She looked hard at Grandmother down the damask cloth. Grandmother stared back, her eyes as cold as crystal. Then Ruby rose, her full majestic height bringing the top of her head almost into collision with the tips of the prisms on the chandelier. Leveling her chin, she said, "One more thing: there's lots of white buy what they want when they can't afford it either—let's give credit where credit is due!" Ruby tossed her head, and then she did graze the chandelier so that, as she fled the room, bits of light broke from the prisms and fell on the tablecloth, scattering rainbows over the cut-glass bowls, over the dinner plates, all over the table. Bubba excused himself and left the room after her. In silence and in trepidation, we watched the last crazy designs from the swinging crystal.

Grandmother, white as the damask, said, "Ruby's that way because her cousin went and got himself killed at Luzon. Don't mind what she says, children—she doesn't know what she's saying."

But Grandfather took exception to her words. "Maude! This has nothing to do with her cousin. This is a matter of philosophy." He sighed. "Ruby has not had your advantages," he said, fixing our mothers, Grandmother, and even us children, with a sad gaze. "She is given to profusion, but she is not wrong." Perhaps if he'd stopped there, things might have been mended, but he went on, stabbing at the relish dish with a pickle fork for emphasis.

"Furthermore, she makes Bubba supremely happy. Let's give credit where credit is due. You *must* mind what she says. Think of it as a gift." He looked at Grandmother, but she refused to meet his gaze. She was tight-lipped and pale. The color had gone from everyone's cheeks. Only a dash of color remained, a small reflection on the table as the prisms shuddered to a halt above our heads.

Lifesaving Lessons

~⌐

"We must, we must, we must increase our busts,"
we chanted, arms moving up and down, Coke bottles clenched in each hand. It was stifling hot in
Elizabeth's room with the door closed, but this was
a secret pursuit. Nobody except our young aunt
Ruby knew about these exercises, which, we prayed,
would give us breasts. She didn't put much faith
in them.

"Things happen when they happen," she told
us. "If you want exercise, you'd be better off swimming."

Elizabeth and I liked to swim, not so much for
the activity as for the lifeguards, one in particular,
our idea of perfection, just out of high school and
going to Fayetteville that fall. For now, he sat on
his perch with limbs like a statue's—thick and per-

fectly formed. When we walked past, we could see pale blonde hair on his calves, more on his chest. We dared each other to speak to him.

"Hey, O.T.," Elizabeth drawled. "Hey" was foreign to me, the Yankee cousin from St. Louis. We said "Hi," and so my salute was slightly off, but O.T. answered anyway.

"Hey, Yankee," he said. "When you girls signin' up for Lifesavin'?"

Lifesaving. We hadn't dreamed we were eligible. We'd watched him instructing Gwendolyn and Mary Beth for the past week, but they were fourteen. We'd observed with longing the way O.T. towed them across the pool to demonstrate rescue, the girls' bodies obediently limp as if half-drowned. The way, after lessons, the girls stepped out of the pool, shedding water, the way O.T. watched their wet ruffling from his reclaimed roost.

Elizabeth and I became brave. Big on Greek gods and goddesses that summer, we'd nick-named O.T. "Apollo" because his skin was bronze. The sailor cap he wore distracted from the image, but we felt that without it, he would look like the Apollo in the encyclopedia at the public library.

This was 1953. You had to go some to see pictures of male bodies, adorned or otherwise. We had found the Britannica a good source, and art books similarly rich in possibility. The librarian had no idea what we were so interested in. Our taste was catholic: it ran to anything explicit, male or female, but there was something furtive about our paging through those books. At any time, the librarian, who had a slight but definite mustache, might loom up silently and startle us by asking, "Finding what you want?"

At Uncle Bubba and Ruby's house, there was yet a better book, a huge coffee-table volume of American paintings. Elizabeth and I each had our favorites, and Ruby didn't mind what we looked at. She was not yet thirty that summer, our youngest great-aunt, and for that reason we didn't "Aunt" her. She exclaimed with us as we turned pages. Frequently we made up stories based on the pictures. The ones we liked best had people in them, and one which always drew us was a Thomas Hart Benton, *The Ballad of the Jealous Lover of Lone Green Valley*. A woman in a pink dress clutched her breast. Blood flowed. A farmer stood before her, dagger in hand, hat tilted. In the foreground, an indifferent trio of musicians played a fiddle and harmonicas, oblivious to the drama behind them.

"Never take up with a jealous man," said Ruby. "Look what can happen to a woman, and nobody does a damn thing about it. That girl is going to bleed to death for sure. And over what? She had a generous and loving nature is all I can see." We shook our heads, sad for that poor woman.

"Another thing," said Ruby, who loved an audience, "never take up with a musician. Look at those men," she pointed to the trio. "In a world of their own, is what."

"And Orpheus," one of us would say, sinking into this lovely afternoon litany, "look what he did to poor Eurydice."

"Don't never look back," said Ruby. "That's what you have to learn from that one."

Here was a man running with a baby in his arms, a ladder against the house behind him. In a hushed voice Ruby told us about the Lindbergh kidnapping. We shivered. We worried. Grandmother's house was low. Our shared room was by the driveway, and sometimes, after dark, men came to the window seeking Grandfather to come out and deliver babies or sew up wounds. We'd got used to those urgent tappings, but what if, some evening, it wasn't a patient but a kidnapper? Ruby laughed.

"Scream bloody murder," she advised. "It would save your life. Unless, of course, there's just musicians around. That poor woman!" She'd flip the pages back to *The Jealous Lover*.

Relieved to have us out of the house visiting Ruby, Grandmother wasn't the slightest bit interested in lifesaving lessons. O.T. had told us his class met every afternoon at 2:00.

"I cannot possibly take you," said Grandmother. "Ask Ruby. She just sits around in that empty house with not a thing to do. No children, and not likely to have them either," she said, pursing her lips. We didn't know what she meant. She was always saying unpleasant things about Ruby even though Bubba was our grandfather's own baby brother. It was as if he and Ruby belonged to someone else's family. Grandmother *had* said, however, that we could ask.

"I'd be tickled pink," Ruby told us, and then, inspired, she drove us down to Bubba's store to pick out new bathing suits. Grandmother and Ruby had completely different tastes. Grandmother's ran to plain tank suits, whereas Ruby liked color and patterns. She thought we'd look cute in two-piece floral prints with ruffled tops, but they were too juvenile. We elected black sarong-style suits. Ruby smiled and said we could have whatever we wanted, but black absorbed all the heat; we'd be more comfortable in a color.

"If you are ever in a desert," she said, "in a big tent with a handsome sheik offering you something to wear on your camel ride to the next oasis . . ." here she paused and lowered her voice. We bent close to hear, there in the side aisle of Bubba's store. A desert sheik. He would look like Robert Taylor. "Choose white robes," Ruby said urgently. "Remember what I'm telling you. It could save your life out there."

"Grandmother will never go for black," said Elizabeth practically. She didn't plan to travel much and tended to see things how they played in Arkansas. "We'll just catch hell," she sighed. It was hard, very hard, to see the justice in life. Here was Ruby offering us any suit we wanted and Bubba himself echoing her generosity, and there was Grandmother's propriety floating like a huge cobweb from the ceiling of their store.

"You can't take bathing suits back," I told Elizabeth. "There isn't a thing she can do if we take them home."

"Boy, are you dumb," said my cousin. "What kind of underwear are you wearing?"

I shrugged. Elizabeth and I wore sturdy white cotton underwear, Lollipops, because Grandmother had firm ideas about intimate apparel. It should never be anything but clean and sensible. We had been shopping the first week of my visit, Grandmother horrified at my skimpy blue nylon panties with their stretched elastic and straggly lace.

"How could your mother have possibly let you go for a visit with underwear like this? Accidents," she continued. "You have to consider accidents. You never want to be hit by a car in dirty underwear." Elizabeth and I pouted. We didn't plan to be hit; we didn't see how Lollipops were going to save our lives if we were run down. Grandmother told us not to be sassy.

We could imagine what she would say when she saw the sarongs. There was no way we could even think of taking home the ones with the tiger print or leopard spots, yet we tried them on, parading around the back of Bubba's store, dashing behind the gray curtain of his changing room whenever we thought a customer was approaching. We vamped, inspected ourselves in the three-way mirror, and looked carefully for any sign of breasts. We sat on the triangular plywood seat in the dressing room and shared a Coke from the machine.

"For the jungle suits, we really ought to have busts," said Elizabeth glumly.

"We don't want to look silly," I agreed. We thought about black absorbing the heat. We selected a white sarong for Elizabeth, a turquoise one for me.

Lifesaving started on Monday. When we began the lessons, Ruby's arms were smooth and white, her shoulders freckled. By the time we finished, triumphantly heaving up a burlap sack weighted with ten pounds of coal from the bottom of the pool, Ruby was freckled all over. "Speckled," she laughed, "like an old barnyard hen."

She wore a tiger-striped suit and a swimming cap with a rubber spangle of fuchsia she said was a mum. We could spot her anywhere in the large pool, just looking for that cap as she swam steadily back and forth a prescribed number of times. Because she was so tall, her arms were long and she moved through the water as if it were her native element. When she swung up onto the cement and pulled off her cap, shaking her head, her whole body shimmered. The tiger stripes waved as she stamped her feet.

O.T. watched her, too, with something like longing on his otherwise inscrutable face, but he was respectful, even though she had told him not to "ma'am" her, it made her feel old.

"He's right cute," she told us as we whispered to each other from our own stretched-out towels, and we giggled agreement, picking at the frayed edges of the towels as we sucked in our tummies, trying to puff out our chests. All that summer we strutted in front of O.T., made countless trips to the Coke machine, did laps, practiced our lifesaving techniques.

"That's right," Ruby assured us, "you learn best by doing. You just keep doin', sugars."

When she took us to the pool, she changed her clothes there in the dressing room so that anyone who wanted could admire her freckled shoulders and hands, her milky white body which sometimes bore mysterious lavender bruises, either on her shoulder just above her breast or sometimes on her neck. She was a downriver goddess.

The passion we felt for O.T. was something she understood, knowing about love. She said it scarcely had to do with the lifeguard himself, but she told us it was natural. O.T. was a triangular shaped fellow with close-cropped hair and broad shoulders, a Noxzema-ed nose wedged onto his face like an afterthought. His sailor cap didn't quite hide the way he watched the older girls, especially Gwendolyn, as she dipped her painted toes into the bleach-water trough you had to walk through to get to the pool from the ladies' dressing room.

It was distasteful as anything, that cloudy white trough, the necessity for it unspoken but ominous. Some people thought going to the pool was the closest thing to heaven, but for me, even though I had begged for lessons, the community pool was

full of reminders about how dangerous the universe was.

Beyond the trough, there were the rows of damp
benches and dark green lockers past which we had to
file. We had put on our bathing suits at home, mod-
estly, but there in the locker room, we saw women
dressing and undressing: pubic hair, fat thighs, sag-
ging breasts with great rose nipples. None of this
did we see at home where everyone dressed behind
closed doors and respected privacy. Here there was
none. The universe did not admit of privacy. That
was something that existed in Grandmother's prim
white house.

There was something terrifying about those
large uncovered female bodies we saw on our way
to the swimming pool, their bulk, their odor, their
ease, a series of laughing women pushing their hair
up into rubber caps, kneading their breasts into the
tops of bathing suits, or peeling their suits off, running their large hands down their sides in a caress
of relief at being out of the boned suits they wore.

Grandmother was slim. Her body encased in
simple linen dresses smelled good, did not bulge or
sigh for release. These bodies seemed to ache for it;
you could tell from the way a large-boned woman
would swing her leg up onto the bench and lather
it with Coppertone. We felt daring just to linger

there without any excuse for our presence, observing them.

In Ruby's book of American paintings, these women leaned over rooftops drying their hair or rested naked against haystacks, while a lecherous farmer peered around a tree in Thomas Hart Benton's *Persephone*. Respectability had its pages too— the girl from Philadelphia all dressed in white, dreamily holding a fan. We described her when Grandmother looked up from her gardening to ask what we'd been doing over at Ruby's all afternoon. And the farm couple by Grant Wood or his group portrait of the Daughters of Revolution. These, Ruby told us laughing, *must* be respectable, so these were what we described, omitting Ruby's gloss on respectability, her stories, our adventures. We had asked the only person we trusted to tell us, the last person Grandmother would have recommended. Ruby was nominally of the older generation because of her marriage to Bubba, yet she seemed caught between.

Elizabeth and I elaborated on our gods and goddesses, Ruby like Persephone, shuttling back and forth between the kingdoms of darkness and light. We and the swimming pool were the light. Bubba's store and all those old people she had to endure, well, they were obviously the dark. But the thing was, traveling back and forth like that, you could learn a lot. Ruby seemed to know everything.

"Ruby," we asked, lying on the dank yellow grass by the pool, trying to get warm after our lesson, "what is it like to be in love?"

She lay on her stomach, her chin on her folded hands. She stared past O.T.'s lifeguard stand, past the poplars at the edge of the chain link fence, seeming to focus on a shadowy place we couldn't discern. What she didn't say was that we would know when it hit us. That we were too young, that it was foolish to ask.

Ruby's hair was auburn, plain red in a certain light, and now, as she stared off into the distance, some of it was almost black from being wet at the nape of her neck. We watched her carefully, eager for what she had to say. We knew about oracles, gypsies, how they told your future, but somehow, even then, we had sense enough to put our money on Ruby.

"It's not like the movies," she said slowly. "It's not really like the books." We knew her for an avid reader. Sometimes she took us to the library where we got books for our summer reading lists.

"You can tell us," we said. "We won't tell." Meaning we wanted to be initiated into the secret club. We wished to know, really know, what we were in for. The mystery of life. We already knew about babies; we'd seen kittens born under the back steps at Grandmother's only last week. Even so, Grandmother wouldn't let us see *From Here to Eternity* at the Uptown Theatre. We were caught too that summer in a frenzied limbo between worlds we didn't quite inhabit. We wanted now, our first summer of adolescence, to know about love.

"Why isn't it in books?"

"Shut up, Elizabeth," I said wearily. I didn't want to know why. I wanted to know what. It. Was. Like. Love. We had been practicing Dead Man's Float while O.T. ferried us across the pool, his impersonal arm crooked across our shoulders and beneath our chins. He was demonstrating how to save someone but we were, one at a time, separately towed and thrilled. Was what we felt, the water parting around us as O.T. swam, was that rippling, spinning pleasure akin to love?

Ruby rolled over on her back, hitched her bathing suit well up over her full breasts, and closed her eyes. Maybe she'd seen something beyond the poplars and the cyclone fence that kept the colored out, something she knew about love out there in the mown field where they set up revival tents and carnival rides whenever they came to town.

"It's like going on the Ferris wheel," she said, "getting on with someone you think is really nice, and the man operating the Ferris wheel kind of winks as you get in. He slams that bar across the two of you, and you're in it together, however it's going to be. When you lurch forward as it's cranking up, maybe you're a little scared 'cause maybe it's one of those hot nights with the threat of storm, but it isn't raining yet, only a hint of it, thunder clouds off in the distance. Maybe you're shivery because of the county fair, all that activity, those big stuffed animals, the penny-pitching jars, the freaks, canned goods in the tent with bright lights. Well, all of it gathers together and then swims under you as you rise in that little compartment for two people, and it all falls away. There aren't, any more, all those crowds. It's quiet and private and you're turning around and around through the air, just the two of you, looking at each other, not seeing everything below, not seeing anything but one another."

She lay very still then and we waited for her to begin again. Behind us, O.T. took his bullhorn and yelled at some kids on the diving board.

"Falling in love is like being suspended on top of the world in that Ferris wheel when the operator has stopped to let someone else on, but you're at the top so you can't tell, and you don't care whether anyone down there is getting on or off. There's just you and him." She sat up and hugged her knees.

"And what it's like down below where Mrs. Smith is in a swivet because Mrs. Brown's fruit cobbler got a blue ribbon, or some kid's balloon twisted to look like a poodle has popped and she's screaming for another, or a carny's trying to lure the youngsters inside to see the contortionist, or Joe Boy is standing in front of the fun-house mirror looking at how he'd look if he didn't look the way he does, what it's like down there with everyone wishing for something they don't have, it doesn't matter at all. *You* have what you want, and that's what counts."

Elizabeth and I were motionless, our faces serious, eyes fixed on Ruby.

"Love is selfish like that. The whole earth could fall away and you wouldn't give a fig. You can look off into the distance, you're eye-level with the clouds, you could pitch lightning into the middle of the cattle pen and cause such havoc! You could stop the thunder and bottle it up, you feel that powerful. You know a storm might make a liar of your feelings, but you don't care. You are on top of the world," she said, unwinding her arms from around her knees and extending her long legs carefully, gracefully, as if she were stepping down from a great height. She lay back, resting on her elbows, studying her painted toenails. She looked at us sitting up expectant and cross-legged at her recital and she smiled.

"You'll see," she said, "you'll see."

"How do you know you're in love?" I asked shyly.

"Well, how do you know you're on top of a Ferris wheel? Doesn't anybody have to tell you that, do they?"

Elizabeth shook her head. "It sure ain't in the books like that."

"Nope, that's a real problem with these books. Still," she said, reaching for her crocheted bag with the wooden handle and pulling out some Dentyne, offering it to us before taking a stick herself, "we'd best be reading anyway."

"Our books aren't due until Friday," I said, "but I've finished mine." I always carried a book to the pool, for what I had observed during the first week of Red Cross instruction was that O.T., for whom I had the most intense desire, didn't even know my name at week's end. Worse, he called me Yankee, and Elizabeth, Squirt. He paid us no attention at all outside of class. Books offered solace. But now, lying on my towel, chewing gum, I thought not about books but about Ferris wheels. I almost always got dizzy and slightly sick with excitement.

Sometimes I was downright scared. I took a deep breath and confessed this.

Elizabeth snorted as if to say she already knew that. Unfortunately she did because I'd thrown up all over the seat when the carnival came to town for the Fourth of July, but Ruby only said that falling in love was kind of like that too.

She stood up then and brushed grass clippings off her legs and looked down at us.

"Nothing in life is a bed of roses," she said. "That Ferris wheel goes up, and it comes down. You got to pay to take the ride."

We stood too, prompted by something in her voice that told us it was time to leave. Carefully we shook our towels so as not to get grass on Bubba's back seat when Ruby drove us home. We slung the towels around our necks and followed her through the loathsome Clorox footbath into the locker room, where we sat on a bench and waited while Ruby showered. She reappeared with her towel around her like Dorothy Lamour.

"Your mamas wouldn't be so pleased with all this conversation about Ferris wheels," she said. "You want to take a survey, you ask them what they think love's like, but don't be quoting me, and don't tell me what they say neither." She took her underwear out of the wire basket in which she'd left it, and gravely we watched as she bent to drop her breasts, like pears, into each cup. Her panties were red nylon with black lace around the legs. Instinctively we knew that hers was not the kind of underwear in which to have an accident.

Sometimes we did errands on our way back from the pool. Not infrequently, we stopped at a nearby orchard for a bushel of fruit. Ruby allowed us each to take a peach and to eat it over our towels as she drove. We'd have to wipe the peaches to remove the fuzz and whatever germs might be resident on their soft skin. In the front, driving rapidly now, Ruby would also eat, her own towel spread over her lap. Once in a while she talked absently to herself, but most often she turned on the radio and we listened to Patti Page, Jo Stafford, and Teresa Brewer as we covered the distance home. Collectively we decided to see the pyramids along the Nile together. We would take Bubba along, seeing how Ruby loved him so much.

"You *do* love Bubba," I wanted to say, watching her face rearrange itself at the suggestion. Jo Stafford had just finished singing, and the air in the car was thick with peach scent and dust from the orchard. Instead, I said nothing, slightly uneasy for a reason I couldn't identify.

The idea of falling in love was exciting, but it seemed to happen to people when they were young, and Ruby and Bubba were scarcely that. It was even more difficult to imagine Grandmother or Daddy Doc in love, or our parents. Although these people surely loved one another, it seemed different from falling in love. I began to see too that what Elizabeth and I wanted from O.T. had more to do with recognition than with love. If a god bowed to you, did it make you some kind of a goddess? If he failed to, might you still be divine? I thought about Diana and the hunt, goddesses in disguise. I longed to be translated into another shape. Breasts would have been a terrific help.

Sometimes instead of going to the orchard, we went to the ice house, and the man on the platform slid back the heavy wooden door, revealing blocks of ice. From where we stood below the platform, he looked like one of the figures in Ruby's painting book. Like the boxers' in the match at Sharkey's, his arms bulged when he took tongs and hefted ice into the trunk of Ruby's car. She always kept newspapers back there, and it was our task to spread the paper quickly before the man brought the slippery ice down from the scales.

Once or twice, we observed another man who seemed to know Ruby. He spoke quietly to her, appearing, it seemed, out of nowhere. The third time we saw him, I noticed that his car had been parked at the ice house when we drove up, as if he was waiting for something, but ice wasn't something you waited around with during the summer in Arkansas.

"Who *is* that?" I asked. Ruby said he was someone she used to know, and now he sold insurance. She spoke in a matter-of-fact, offhanded manner, but Elizabeth and I were so full of romance and love and our futile obsession with O.T., that we teased her. "He loves you, doesn't he?"

"He's just sitting here waiting in case you need ice," I added. "I saw him here last time."

"Nonsense," said Ruby sharply. "It's coincidence, is all. John Clay's married with two kids," she said. Her voice rocked a little then. "They got an ice-cream maker like I do. Probably their kiddies like peach ice cream just as much as you two." She spun the car away from the ice house so rapidly that gravel rattled beneath her tires. After that, I was sorry I'd said anything, for we never saw the man there again. I remembered he was as tall as she was, rather dark, and much younger than Bubba, closer to Ruby's age. Although he looked nothing like O.T., he too carried himself proud. He had a distinctive chin, sharp and cleft.

Years later, when Bubba died, I saw him again, at the funeral. I'd been away myself for close to thirty years, and I'd taken a ride or two on Ferris wheels. When we returned from the cemetery, that same man was at Ruby's house with a woman who must have been his wife. She was looking around like someone burnt up with curiosity. I saw her finger Ruby's Hummel figurines on the mantelpiece, watched her turn over a tea cup to see the pattern. All the while, her husband never took his eyes off Ruby, who was receiving friends and neighbors on the sofa. I found Elizabeth in the dining room pouring tea and asked her, since she had lived all her life there in that small town.

"John Clay? One thing I'll say for you, you don't miss much, never did."

"Who is he? I think I've seen him, but where?"

"Ruby's *friend*. She was engaged to him—not really, but in a way—before the war. Then she fell in love and married Bubba." I took a cup from Elizabeth, looking back into the living room across the china rim, blowing softly on the hot tea before I sipped. I have never needed to haul anyone up from the bottom of a pool nor even tow someone across an expanse of water. All that preparation had been for naught. I have never been even remotely near the scene of a water accident.

Of course I have, as everyone has, passed people and ambulances on highways. Because of Grandmother, I almost always hope they have clean underwear, as if that fact might save them from the consequences of their wrong turns, the slick pavement, whatever in the troubled universe has brought them to that sad moment.

Standing next to Elizabeth and the tea cups, I saw John Clay's wife fingering a silver frame with Bubba's picture in it. A small thick woman with fat ankles, she was apparently nearsighted but too vain to wear her glasses, for she brought the picture close to her face. She looked entirely respectable, like one of those women holding a tea cup in that Grant Wood painting.

I hadn't thought of that picture book in years, yet here in the house where Elizabeth and I had pored over its pages so many afternoons, the images came back. Ruby, subdued, alone for a moment in the midst of the funeral company, an hour back from the cemetery, laid her head against the sofa and looked around the room. John Clay gazed hungrily at her, like that Thomas Hart Benton farmer peering around the tree at the country goddess who'd stripped off her clothes in the summer heat. Ruby met his gaze. Although her hair had silver strands after all these years, she still looked like Persephone, full of life and just back from the kingdom of the dead.

Ducks

"Bubba," said Ruby, looking over from her television program, "do you think I look like Dolly Parton?"

Bubba was approaching his seventy-fifth birthday with all the wariness of a hunter. He protected himself on all sides and generally lay low, telling himself it wasn't damp, just cold. Ruby, his wife, was coming up on sixty, but if Bubba was pulling in, Ruby was continuing to expand, looking around as if the world was new and she had just come into the garden. Clairol kept her hair the color of autumn leaves. Lavish creams kept her skin soft—Bubba had always liked her freckles.

"Sugar," he said carefully, "Dolly's pretty, and she sure can sing up a storm, but she ain't a patch on you."

"Bubba," Ruby persisted, "you mean that? We're about the same age. I went to a dance once with one of her kin. She might have been there herself, downriver."

They were coming in low now, the sun just shimmering above the horizon, the silhouettes of the ducks black against the dark streaked sky. It looked easy, Bubba thought, but you could miss even at this close range. You could wound a bird and lose it in the marsh; bad business. Nothing was certain except that Dolly was too young to have been at any summer dance with Ruby.

"Sugar," he said, "*I* was at a dance once with Dinah Shore and her sister. Doc and Maude were there too. Did I ever tell you?"

"Yes, I do believe you did." She shifted in her armchair. "I thought we'd have dinner up at the club, and you can stay on afterwards for your poker game. I will just occupy myself with Martha Nell and then come back for you."

Bubba frowned. Martha Nell was Ruby's sister, but he'd never trusted her. She had left town to marry and divorce twice before coming back to town with a questionable son, Frank, who lived out in San Francisco.

"What call you got to visit Martha Nell? Nothing but trouble over there, the way I hear it."

Ruby stretched her legs long before her and crossed her ankles, a gesture he had always liked. "Beats television," she said simply. She stood up, tugged her sweater down over her waist. "Tell you the truth, honey, sometimes I miss the store. People to talk to. But it was time," she added. "I know it was time. We didn't want to spend the rest of our lives behind a counter, now, did we?"

Oh, he thought, now we're going to talk about taking a trip some place we've never been. Vegas or something. He could feel it in the air just the way he could sense the birds coming in. Six months since they'd sold the store; he was surprised, in a way, that it had taken her this long.

Bubba sat squarely in his chair, one hand spread over each upholstered arm, bracing himself for her proposal, his salt and pepper hair neatly combed, his fine cotton shirt starched, his tie in place. He sat patiently, his eyes glittering as Ruby moved to the walnut desk, pausing to adjust the drapery. "I want you to look at these brochures." She stuck out her lip. "If I can find them," she added, rummaging through the papers on the desk. Very reluctantly she drew a pair of glasses from her skirt pocket. "Oh, here," she smiled.

"I don't mind," Bubba smiled up at her. "There's some life in the old boy yet, huh?" He reached up and slipped his hand beneath her sweater. Ruby sat on the edge of his chair like a silky Persian cat. She ruffled his hair.

"I was thinking we could make it a birthday trip, to Maui or someplace romantic like that."

"I thought you wanted to go to Vegas."

"No, Maui, Hawaii, as in *Magnum P.I.*, you know. We wouldn't have to go through Honolulu unless we wanted to."

"You don't want to go to Honolulu?" She always had something to surprise him. Always, like the time she'd picked herself up and stormed out of Maude and Doc's house over some foolishness of Maude's. Ruby was so tall that she'd jangled the crystals on Maude's imported chandelier that afternoon. Later the same week, she'd removed the glass chandelier from their own dining room and replaced it with a brass one.

"I could have hurt myself," she explained. "I wouldn't want to make the same mistake twice."

"Are you thinking of storming out of here?" he'd asked her mildly.

"Aw, Bubba," she said, "brass is easier than crystal anyway. Don't bother yourself about it, honey."

But he had bothered about it now for over thirty years. The way she took Maude on over a matter of philosophy, whether or not you should live for today or store up for tomorrow, buy cash on the line or on credit. The way Maude had of measuring everything, whereas Ruby measured little. Maude did not forgive Ruby the scene at her dinner table.

"Fiddledeedee," said Ruby. "I don't forgive her either!"

Bubba and Doc had continued to go duck hunting together, had managed well enough all these years in spite of the breach between their wives. Their old mother, Miss Sissie, had given up efforts at peacemaking, inviting Ruby and Bubba for cards on alternate Mondays, Maude and Doc on other evenings. It was only at Passover, Bubba thought, when Maude held the family seder, that he felt at all sorry for the rift. Ruby was a Baptist, and try as she might, her matzo balls were hard as lead shot. Since they had no children, and the seder seemed senseless to Bubba if you couldn't share it, they had given it up at his suggestion.

Ruby loved ceremonies. "I could invite people," she protested. "Really, I'd be pleased to," she said, but Bubba hadn't the heart to see her work so hard trying to turn carp into gefilte fish. He'd rather gut catfish and deep fry them with her, create their own ceremony, with Jack Daniel's instead of Mogen David.

"We're not converts, sugar," he told her. "I don't want you to be anything but yourself." When she worked in his store, her red hair had flamed behind the counter where she stood in slippers to wait on farm folks on Saturdays. Now it was rusty and bound into a coil, and he had watched her humor his mother who had outlived even Maude. Ruby watched television with his mother, describing the characters' clothes and events with great tact, as Sissie had lost her vision. Although Sissie had been dead for several years, Bubba could still hear Ruby's commentary.

"Angela now, she's got on a white suit, long sleeves, a huge slit, high heels," she'd begin, and Sissie would interrupt,

"You should have seen her in *Johnny Belinda*."

"You have such a good memory," Ruby would say patiently. No one after all these years said boo to Bubba about marrying outside the faith. His mother had gone so far as to suggest she change her name to Ruth because she had earned it, but Ruby said it was hard enough to know who she was without getting confused when people called her. Shyly she had been reading the Old Testament, Bubba had seen her, looking for what might have prompted Sissie to mention Ruth.

Bubba loved her for that, loved her for present charity and past endurance, especially for the day years ago when she stood up to Maude on behalf of all the colored in town, telling her the dumbest one of them was smarter than Maude, who was always measuring what couldn't be quantified. Bubba worshiped Ruby, even though he feared that one day he might incur her wrath, and that she might storm out on him, all because of their brass chandelier.

"Why, you followed me out," she laughed. "I could never leave you after that. I could never leave you anyway." She kissed the top of his head, for she towered above him. "I love you, Bubba, more than anyone else."

He had been content with that, ignoring occasional unaccountable absences. She always came back to him, and she arrived punctually to pick him up from his poker game, leaving her bright red Cadillac parked in front of the country club in the no-parking zone in order to meet him inside the lobby. From the card room he saw her, majestic in her ankle-strapped heels and her knit dress, a loop of gold dangling from each ear, more gold at her throat. With his merchandiser's eye, Bubba approved the cut of her skirt, its stylish length, the way it hung from her hips.

"Ruby's here," Doc said. He had always liked her. "Time to close up shop."

"Doc," Ruby greeted him, "you haven't come to dinner in too long."

"Don't eat much these days."

"Well, I don't cook much, so you come on over. Bubba and I got a freezer full of catfish, and I know you'll eat that."

"How was Martha Nell?" Bubba asked as she chauffeured him and Doc in the back seat down the steep country club drive.

"She's in a regular swivet. Frank's out in California sick as a dog with some kind of pneumonia. I think I heard of it on *Donahue*," she added, lowering her voice. "I think it means—you know."

"I'm glad I retired," said Doc. "I don't even read my journals lately. I wouldn't know how to treat it. Not that we're apt to see much of it here. People like Frank, they mostly head to California, don't stay home."

"Maybe it's just plain pneumonia," said Bubba cautiously. "Frank is a good boy." Bubba and Ruby had taken Frank fishing every summer of his life until he moved to California. Bubba and Doc had taken Frank duck hunting with them, taught him how to shoot cleanly, carefully. He and Ruby had given him a job in the store in high school. He was as close to a child of their own as they had ever had.

~⌒~

Home seemed far away a few weeks later as Bubba and Ruby settled into their hotel room in Union Square. Bubba had bought a package deal, and he and Ruby were on their way to Maui, breaking the journey at her suggestion with two days in San Francisco.

"Let's call Frank and invite him to dinner," said Ruby as soon as the bellhop had set down their luggage and left the room.

"I want to take a nap," said Bubba. "I don't want to see Frank. Not unless Martha Nell sends for him. *Then* I'll visit him." By now he had read the *Reader's Digest* and *Time*, and he was convinced that Frank was contagious in spite of what Doc had told him.

Ruby put her hands on her hips and shook her head. "Shame," she said. "Shame on you, Bubba D."

"He's no kin of mine," said Bubba.

"That child has called you Uncle Bubba since he could talk. He's *our* nephew."

"He's not. And I don't want to borrow trouble."

"We've missed a lot of trouble," said Ruby, "not having children of our own. We can't duck this, honey. Martha Nell wrote him we were coming."

"Breakfast," said Bubba heavily. He knew when he was beat. "Breakfast tomorrow, not dinner."

They arranged to meet Frank in the coffee shop, and Bubba sat stirring his tea nervously, feeling the draft from the revolving door every other moment. Finally, he looked up to see Frank, pale and thin as a mannequin, hurrying toward them. Frank bent to kiss them each, and Bubba's heart pounded. He ducked his head into Frank's chest and smelled the English Leather they always sent him for holidays. Suddenly he had an image of Frank in loose shorts and cowboy boots standing in Bubba's bathroom squirting shaving cream into the bathtub while Bubba shaved. The times they had had together. Why, with no man in Martha Nell's house, he, Bubba, had taught Frank to raise the toilet seat. Tears stung his eyes. He blew his nose as Frank sat down.

"Darlin'," said Ruby, "you look handsome in that suit."

"I've been sick; I guess Mama told you," said Frank, looking into their eyes for confirmation, but Bubba continued to hide his face in his handkerchief.

"Off to Hawaii for your birthday, Uncle Bubba?"

"A big one," said Bubba, recovering. "Seventy-five. Have to keep up with this young'un," he joked.

"How's Mama? How's her garden?"

"We played cards last week," said Ruby. "Her garden is fine, only it needs more looking after. Maybe if you were to go home, help her out a bit . . . she'd love to see you."

"Lost a little weight there, haven't you, Frank?" Bubba took a more direct line.

"I had pneumonia, but now I'm fine. I am so glad to see you, Uncle Bubba, Ruby." Frank drummed his fingers on the table. "Last month, the Stevenses were out here—they didn't even call. I went all through school with Gwen and Douglas, and they didn't call."

"Maybe they phoned and you were out, Frank," said Ruby.

"I have an answering machine," he said bitterly. "Mama wrote me they were coming; she told them to call."

"Maybe she thought she told them. Your mama gets confused sometimes," said Ruby. "She'd sure like to have you home, Frank."

"I'd like to see her, but I don't know . . ." Frank's voice trailed off. "I had to miss some work when I was sick. I don't have any vacation time coming right now. Maybe in a few months."

"Fiddlededee," said Ruby. "Seize the day! Martha Nell would like to see you *now*."

"Ruby," said Bubba, "we have to leave soon if we're going to visit Chinatown. Today's the only full day we have to see the sights," he said to Frank.

"I work right nearby," said Frank. "I'll go as far as Grant Avenue with you so you won't get lost. This is an easy town to get lost in—look at me." His voice dropped. He stared at them both. "I'm going to die."

Ruby had been blotting her lipstick on the paper napkin as he spoke. She pulled the paper away and Bubba saw the imprint of her lips, a bright red startled "O" on the paper. Slowly she raised her eyes to Frank. Her mouth reshaped itself.

"Nonsense. Well, that is, we're all going to die some day, isn't that right, Bubba?" Bubba couldn't speak, but he wanted to scream "No! no!" *He* didn't have plans for dying yet, and Frank, why it was obscene, a young handsome man like this, it was impossible.

Ruby rose up to her full majestic height and came around the table. She folded Frank into her arms.

"You just need a little fattening up, some home cooking," she said. She held him close, looking at Bubba frozen in his chair. "You're not lost, sweetheart. We'll figure out something. I just know we will. Now," briskly, "I have a date with some shops in Chinatown. Bubba, pay the man. Let's go."

⁓

"I'm so glad we came, Bubba," said Ruby when Frank had left them to walk downhill to his office. "Look at those apartments there. That's where I would live if we lived here," she said, waving across toward Telegraph Hill. "Right under that tower there, looking over the water." She squeezed his arm. "I'm going to let you buy me a silk kimono, a red one with dragons on it."

Bubba marveled at how quickly she got on with living. Frank was barely alive. He had been mannerly, funny about life here in San Francisco, but his cheeks were so hollow that the bones seemed to hold up his eyes. His face looked like Death.

"What about Frank?" Bubba asked. "What are you going to tell Martha Nell?"

Now he saw that the trip to Hawaii had been part of a larger scheme, celebrating his birthday only one component. Bubba was content with his life, wary only at what threatened its even keel. What if you shot at a duck and a vulture came down instead?

But now Ruby was laughing and pulling him along past a store whose windows were hung with dead ducks strung up by their ankles. "I'm going to figure out some way to get that boy home," she said. "Martha Nell will spring for his fare, that's the easy part. The hard part is getting past the fear. He's got some living yet to do. That boy needs to feel important." Then she saw the Peking ducks hanging in the window.

"Let's get one and take it back to our hotel. I do believe they'll cut it up for us," and there she was, asking and receiving, and the duck with its greasy anise perfume was tucked into a carton and a brown bag before Bubba could say Tums. Next door was a shop in which Bubba found himself surveying a rack of kimonos with a practiced eye. They were not made very well, but they were not marked up excessively. Bubba looked over the inventory, figuring from habit what he could have sold in Arkansas. There were baskets stacked in the aisles, baskets woven in the shapes of roosters, baskets fashioned like mallards, tiny baskets labeled "for crickets." He never could have sold those, Bubba thought, although people were superstitious the world over. As if you could trap good luck and bring it to your hearth. He shook his head. You had to woo your luck, create it carefully. He had deliberately married Ruby, perhaps his single act of defiance—and like a lucky cricket, she had brought him happiness beyond all expectation.

Bubba stood behind her watching her hold up a piece of blue silk and then, deftly, substitute a red one that made her hair gleam in the dark shop. At his elbow, the old proprietor, his face smooth as almonds, regarded her too. A scratched mirror tilted against a column in the middle of the aisle gave back reflections of them all, Ruby larger than life itself, clutching at the colored silk, and behind her, the two old men. Bubba saw that they were old, and yet the mirror seemed magic, and for a moment he saw Ruby as she had been forty years ago and himself as a slim young man in a straw hat, and even the old proprietor as he must have appeared once, sleek and youthful, making his way in the New World. How odd, he thought, that I should look so old and feel so young.

"How long you been here?"

"Born here."

"Right here? Chinatown? I swan," Bubba said.

"More than twenty years, I lived in one room with my family. Now, I have two sons, an engineer from U.C. Berkeley and an architect. We live in Seacliff. It's another world. My sons live in the East Bay. Do your children live near you?"

"No children," Bubba said sadly.

Ruby pivoted on one toe, spinning the silk toward Bubba. He nodded, "It suits you, darlin'."

"Very sad," said the proprietor. "Still," he added, "a fine wife."

"Thank you," Bubba said politely.

"My wife won't wear anything from my store. You have a store too?"

Bubba nodded.

"I can tell. The way you look at things. My wife only shops at Magnin's, retail. Sometimes Loehmann's. You got Loehmann's where you live?"

Bubba shook his head. "I'm not familiar with the name."

"Discount. Designer labels. They cut them out."

"My wife would like that," Bubba said, and in the mirror they made a face together at their common fate, and Bubba saw how alike they were. Something close to happiness filled his heart. He told the man what a pleasure it was to meet him, and he stood and looked at the man's sons' graduation pictures, which hung behind the cash register, and he was happy for the man's pride. "You ever get to Arkansas, you come and see us," he said.

~⌒

"Ruby," Bubba sighed, leaning back on the giant-sized bed in their room at the St. Francis, as he watched her preen before the mirror in her red silk robe, "you sure do know how to make a man happy."

He sipped on his bourbon and wiped his mouth with a napkin from room service. The duck had an exotic flavor he had never tasted before, and he was glad they had bought it. The purchase seemed daring, somehow, and made him feel young again. Deliberately he had not taken his blood pressure pills that morning. They depressed his normal functioning, and he wanted to be amorous and able for Ruby while they were in San Francisco. His pulse seemed a little fast, but they had had a wonderful afternoon. He wouldn't think about Frank.

"Remember how cute that Frank was when he used to work for us?" Ruby was wistful. "Used to bring me up a frosty Coke from the machine, unpack a carton of Ship 'N Shore blouses faster than I could do it myself, tag them, put them on hangers, so cheerful a boy, who would have thought?"

"A good boy," Bubba agreed. They fell silent remembering Frank at seventeen. How was it that so much promise had disintegrated into this? Bubba privately thanked the Lord that he had no issue of his own to bring him grief of this order. Grief once removed was painful enough. Poor Martha Nell.

Bubba dozed and dreamed while Ruby sat at the desk repainting her nails. The familiar scent of her polish remover made him think he was at home, and he was startled, upon waking, not to recognize his surroundings. A faint odor of anise lingered on his fingers, and the silhouette of an unfamiliar bedside lamp confused him. Beyond the lamp there was a patch of light across the room where Ruby sat blowing on her nails.

Ruby was frowning at the television. "Guess who was on a talk show just before the news and who's lost fifty pounds? Dolly, that's who. She looks years younger. I'm going on a diet when we get home, yes siree bobtail." She picked up her emery board.

Bubba's chest grew tight as it did when he was hunting with Doc and the odor of neat's-foot oil and death filled his nostrils. It made him feel ten or eleven again, the age he had been when he and Doc had witnessed a man shot in a hunting accident. The man had been careless, stepping out in front of the others just as ducks flew over low and veered suddenly left, causing their father to aim and shoot just as the man moved the wrong way. The pain arced through his chest locking him in its embrace. Bubba remembered the dark stain on the man's upper back, the way the water had edged over his jacket as the stain spread outward to meet it, the way his Remington had fallen into the water. The man had pitched sideways after it, lying there a few feet beyond the place where he and Doc crouched helpless to alter the course of events.

He always thought back on that time in the duck blind as when Doc had decided to become a doctor, so as never to be helpless like that again. He himself had decided, although a mere boy, to join the family enterprise and set up a store of his own, never to be called upon to do more than provide clothing for people.

Rousing himself, he decided to send Frank a handsome robe from the men's shop in the lobby. A burst of licorice rose in his throat. This pain, he thought, was from the unfamiliar duck, but it escalated now as he lay propped on an elbow gazing at Ruby across the room. He watched her tap her emery board on the glass top of the table, and he saw her lips form words, but there was such a song in his head, a hymn of pain, that it was all he could do to say, "Ruby, I think I'm going to spoil our trip."

Now the pain enlarged itself and radiated like the several arms of the brass chandelier at home. He had experienced small pains before that caught his breath, but never anything so bothersome that he had told Doc. He shouldn't have eaten the duck; surely, he thought, it was the duck.

In a dish on the nightstand were the inedible parts of the Peking duck they had set aside, feet and the head. The head was dried and shriveled with an eye that seemed to stare hard in his direction, its mouth shut dry in a futile grin. All these years he'd worried about Ruby leaving him, and here he was leaving her alone in a strange city. With a clarity of vision seldom permitted him, like adding all the due bills and accounts and having them tally properly, Bubba did a quick assessment. Ruby would be all right on her own. *She* had really taken care of him. It wasn't the other way around.

Bubba had a sudden vision of Frank coming to the hotel to help Ruby pack his things, hollow-cheeked Frank making arrangements to ship his body home. *He* would be the way that Frank got home again, he saw that, and as Ruby, understanding now that something had gone very wrong, began to run across the room waving her hands, Bubba lay back down, for they were coming in now, lower still, and very dark against the sky.

Sugar Dust

Seems like my whole life has been waiting for something terrible to happen. After my best friend, Claude, and I enlisted, brave for a minute and a half, I had to fight for years to keep my chin up, not to duck. Over there, something bad was always happening, Claude dead before we reached the beach. After that, I waited for it to happen to me, but no bullet with my name on it. I got hit when I got home.

Ruby had married another guy. Not even a fellow like us, but an older man. I don't know. I can still recall the night I stepped off the train, duffel bag over my shoulder, the platform hot and dusty, katydids scraping their legs together. Crickets, they were my Welcome Home band. My folks didn't have a phone downcountry. Nor did Ruby. But when I hiked on out there, went first before even going home, the place was shut up. She was gone.

She was right here, moved into town, and I'd been so near and didn't know it. All my life so close, right here, and yet. The bullets that caught Claude zinged past me, throwing pocks of sand around us, dusting my trousers, the sand caking Claude's clothing where the life drained out, lying there, me alive, him dead, two farm boys from Arkansas, halves of a whole, never at that moment closer or farther apart. A pattern I thought I'd never experience again, that close and far apart business, and yet. And yet, which is why I feel like all my life is spent waiting for something terrible, when what has been most awful has already occurred, just whizzing past my ear.

Maybe if Claude had been there to read between the lines of Ruby's letters, I'd have seen it coming, but I was never any good at reading between the lines. If a person said something, then that was that. Only afterwards, I got good at what wasn't said. I called it my G.I. education. Too late. Ruby gone, wrapped in respectability. Married to a storekeeper, a Jewish one at that. Made me want to join the Klan or something, but hell, when I poked around, there wasn't a soul didn't have a kind word about him. How could I stir up trouble for Bubba, who everybody liked? If I'd known him well at all, I'd probably have ended up liking him myself.

I was that ignorant. Only a tad over twenty when I got back. Went round to the shop where Ruby did manicures only to learn she was working at Davidson's. Tore over there. Saw her ring, saw her whole self changed and not changed all at once. My life, the way I'd planned it, over. Dusted up, done with, along with my long wait for something to happen, and me not even realizing how terrible it would be even in the damned middle of it. Like if you're in a car on the highway and you spin out and all you can do to steer into it and not do the wrong thing. You can't stop to think—not even for a split second or you'll be dead—how terrible it *might* be. That kind of after-the-fact tremble when your knees go to water and you realize how close you were to losing it.

I've been water-kneed since 1944, damned if I haven't, no matter that I went to school and got a degree and came back to open an insurance agency one block down from Davidson's. Shoot, town so small in those days anywhere I set up shop I would've been one block from Davidson's. And get to see her every day of my adult life, my desk angled just so I could look down the street, watch when she pulled her car into the side lot before going to work. Ruby always had her own car—he was good to her—and she always came to the store at ten-thirty, an hour and a half after he opened.

In the beginning, I had this notion to do him harm. I could never have hurt Ruby. I loved that woman. She was half my soul, but if I could have got rid of her husband in his fancy Hickey Freeman suits and his starched white shirts, if I could have found a way to have that door explode on him as he turned the key in the lock, I would have done it. I would. Nobody would have known. Except Ruby, she would have, and then I would have lost her completely, and I couldn't have stood that.

No, all I could do was steal time with her, bide my own time, marry Rita Wilson, raise a family and tend my business, waiting for Bubba to die a natural death, and so, my whole life, wait for it to happen. Which is now. He is dead. I am going to leave my family and marry Ruby as soon as she thinks it decent.

And what if she says no? How could she?

One thing I know. She cannot throw away the past forty years of living with Bubba just like that, but she can't turn her back on the times we had either.

I am talking times the last forty years, not only the times before the war. At first, how we would meet was accidental. People collide in a small town like ours; you can't hardly help it. And then more deliberately, like knowing she would be stopping off at the ice man's, having her squirty little nieces in the car, just getting in a word or two of where and when we'd meet.

Claude, Lord, if he'd been alive, he would have been happy to help us out. His folks, the Todds, still had the farm, and every time I had business out that direction, I'd stop in to see how they was doing. Lonesome out there, up at four, too tired by supper to see straight. Claude's daddy was kin to Ruby's mother, gave her an excuse to visit years after Claude himself had gone to his reward. They knew what we was up to but they never raised an eyebrow. They had expected us to marry, and this was just a proof to them that they, not life, had been right.

"Set some lines out," Mr. Todd would say, "take a li'l break now, John Clay. You workin' too hard, son." Called me son until the day he died. I had become their substitute for Claude. Didn't bother me none. Made me feel how a man might feel when someone addresses him affectionately, "son" meaning long association, meaning boy, I knew you when.

But when Mr. Todd would say that, it was Ruby's cue to stand up and say she'd have to be getting back. We always went downcountry in separate cars. Then we'd meet down by the Todds' stretch of river, beyond the pasture of that damned wall-eyed mule of theirs, yonder from the levee in a tangle of honeysuckle and passion, just where we used to go when we were young. Beneath each other's skin like chiggers, the worse you scratched, the worse the itch until you would want to claw your own self into numbness.

After a few years, we were too old for that. Ruby didn't like the way the mule looked at her, and the weather was too uncertain. Rainy days, the mud could choke a goat. We began to meet in motels afternoons as far away from here as we could drive. New Orleans once.

I see her now. Lovely, long legs draped over a barstool at a coffee and beignet place, laughing, lipstick rimming her cup. Always I think lipstick, I smell perfume, I feel her fine red hair through my fingers. And that day, powdered sugar from the doughnuts dusting her chin.

I reached to dab it off with my little doohickey of a paper napkin.

"Don't," she said, pushing my hand away.

I was surprised. "You want a sugar beard?" I asked. "Suit yourself."

"No, it's just such a married thing to do and we are not."

"What we been up to back in the hotel, that isn't?"

She set down her cup, chicory spilling like dark oil all over the counter. "That most definitely isn't. That is—illicit. It is what I can't help. John Clay, it is getting out of control. I think we'd best stop now, while we can."

The powdered sugar still on her chin. I wanted to lick it off. I wanted to touch her so, but I leaned over my own cup of coffee there in the French Market place. This would have been 1958, I remember because I had been in the insurance business a full ten years, that was why I was attending the convention in New Orleans, but I didn't yet know other insurance men like I do now, so not being with my wife, but with Ruby, they would have no way of knowing. That's how I fix it in my mind, the first convention, the best one, because Ruby had come along. I don't know what she cooked up to tell Bubba, but she came.

And now she was calling it off, our years of being together. For me, those times together were like getting to stop and haul out of the river where all the time in between I was swimming upstream, with no rest, the times with her just the briefest respite from the swimming, the only chance to catch my breath. I thought I would drown.

One of the car companies was advertising "Suddenly it's 1960, 1960 on wheels." I could feel that slogan in my ears, roaring like the future, sleek and polished and empty.

"No," I told her, "it's too late."

"Yes," she said firmly. "I love Bubba and I cannot be running off on him with you. This—" she gestured around us at the market, sacks of coffee slung on the floor, and across the way, huge trucks loading and unloading their cargo, "this is just too damned colorful, John Clay. How am I supposed to go back home and forget it? Forget waking up in that fancy hotel room with the turquoise drapes to match the spread and the sun shimmering through the curtains making diamonds in the air? And us in bed? It is too overwhelming. Not steadying. It will knock me clean off-keel." She shook her head.

I'd overplayed my hand. Showering her with everything grand, trying to outdistance Bubba, I'd gone too far ahead.

"How can I wake up in my own bed with my own thoughts and not remember this?" Ruby smoothed one of her fingernails with another, as if reshaping it with an invisible emery board. She was always fiddling with her nails, but it never irritated me, not even then. My wife's hands are square and short, and she keeps her nails that way, too. I imagine Rita's hand on one side, Ruby's on the other, and it is like two halves *not* of the same thing at all, but utterly different, so much so that their two hands couldn't clap if they had to.

"No," she continued, brushing her own hands, shaking sugar from them, "I got to go on home and try to be normal like everybody else. Faithful. Get you out of my system once and for all. We are thirty-five years old, John Clay. We are old enough to know better."

Now I was roused. "Thirty-five," I took her hand and turned it over as if I was one of those palm readers whose signs we'd passed in the French Quarter. "I see a long life still ahead," I told her, just a little of my oiled insurance voice in my assurance. "Lives intertwined, still half our lives to live, girl. We were supposed to be—" I stopped. She did love her husband. I knew that. It wasn't as if she'd married him out of desperation or something. I was gone in the war, and she fell in love with him. Ruby always had a generous nature. Bad timing was all. But I'd be damned if I'd give up easy.

"I will be with you in the end," I told her quietly. "I will wait." She knew what I meant. She still had sugar on her chin.

Bubba was about fifty then, and I thought that was old. I figured he'd die any day. For someone who studied actuarial tables, I was pretty unrealistic, but that's what passion does. It blindsides you and then it makes you disregard what is right in front of your nose. I couldn't see no more than the Todds' mule.

I took her to the train station, and she went back home to her married life. Miserable, I stayed on at my convention and didn't come home for another four days. It wasn't how I'd planned it, not at all. I had intended for that trip to cement us. I was busier than a one-legged man in a butt-kicking contest arranging it, plotting it out, wining and dining her, having champagne in our room when we arrived, everything. And it had been too much. Better off sticking close to home, the ordinary sneaking off that just required a little lie here or there, nothing grand.

I still saw her every day from my desk, but my kids were starting junior high school, and Rita decided to work in the office. She thought she was doing me a favor and having a career at the same time. This was about the time Jackie Kennedy was beautifying the White House. Every woman in Arkansas who could afford it was needlepointing and mail-ordering wallpaper from Memphis to make their houses look like Jackie's. Rita was avid about decorating, but the only way she could afford it was to earn the money, and wouldn't nobody be foolish enough to hire her but me.

She was good with figures. She was like Ruby that way, mentally quick. She liked mothering, was discontent after they went to school. Work was a good thing for her, and the business did well. We insured colored, for one thing. Rita was smart. She wasn't uppity—I couldn't have married an uppity woman—but she was limited in a way, didn't want them in the schools with our kids.

"What's so special about our kids?" I asked her. "Think they're any different than anybody else's?" When Governor Faubus stood out there on the steps in Little Rock, we fought about it. You couldn't not love a woman you lived with, the mother of your own children, for wanting to protect them, but I swear, I knew Ruby would have been on *my* side. I began to love Rita a little less. I don't know. Lots of people don't vote the same way as their husbands or their wives, and they seem to get along, but integration, it just seemed so logical to me and so awful threatening to Rita, it seemed to stand for how really far apart we were. How close I was to Ruby, only we weren't seeing each other during that spell.

There was the music, every song on the damned radio filled with longing and heartbreak. Almost made me change over to the classical station, but I hate a violin worse'n a cat.

I'd wake up thinking of Ruby, how she looked
sleeping, and I'd look across the pillow at Rita and
want to cry. I could have written a song or two myself. I understood then what Ruby meant and why it
was we had to stop. Rita was pretty then, with gray
eyes and blonde hair, but she looked hard when she
slept, like somebody who'd as soon run you over as
go around, and only when she was awake and could
arrange herself to look easier did I like to look at
her. She knew it too, generally slept with her back to
me. Lord knows what she knew.

She let herself go. Now she's heavy and she
keeps her hair that uniform blonde that waitresses
have; her eyesight is poor. She wears thick glasses
with feminist frames. She is a person whose worst
expectations are always realized, and so she is never
disappointed. I could leave her tomorrow and never
regret it.

Only tomorrow is Bubba's funeral. Damned if
he didn't make seventy-five. I have to laugh when I
think how I misjudged that man. New Orleans so
long ago, we been through Kennedy's assassina-
tion and Vietnam, and drugs here at home as much
as anybody's got anywhere. I don't know what the
world is coming to. My own grandchildren are
starting school now. Rita voted for Ronald Reagan.

Wanted me to put up campaign banners in the office window, but I refused.

I am in the Kiwanis, Mr. Respectability myself. I will attend the funeral. After all, in a small town like this, Davidson's just down the street, of course I knew him. And if we didn't go, what would Ruby think?

Afterwards, we'll do what everybody else does, go back to their house to stand around with cold ham and JELL-O salad and drinks. I believe they're the kind of Jews eat ham, and Ruby never was a convert anyway.

We'll offer our condolences, only I will be celebrating. Jubilation. My face will be like those comedy/tragedy masks the high school always prints on the program, and Lord, we had to go to a mess of those plays, what with all our kids. Two halves of a whole, signifying there's a drama on. You will not be able to tell what is going on behind my nose. Finally it has come to pass, and I will go where I have never set foot before, in their house. I will see with my own two eyes what I have been up against, and I will be able to tell then what to do.

Rita is from Hayes. She knows Ruby and I were high school sweethearts, but she has never understood why our two families never socialized.

"This town is full of people who used to be sweethearts," she told me once. "If they didn't go to the same parties, why there wouldn't be anyone left to dance." Probably she thinks it's because Bubba was a Jew, but since he belonged to the country club and we never did, I don't know how she carries that notion. "He is old," I told her, "has his own crowd."

At our thirtieth high school reunion, we were all at the same dance. It was at their club, the only one in town.

It was during Watergate. Everybody was taking bets on who would go to jail. We were all rooting for Martha Mitchell since she was from Pine Bluff. John Mitchell, he seemed so old to us, and I remember thinking, "*We* are the old ones now, thirty years out, Claude dead longer than he was alive. He was eighteen, and that now thirty years ago." Funny reunion arithmetic. I looked across the room at where Rita was talking with some of her friends and realized I had been married more than half my life to her. Started out betting on John Mitchell, joking about how he had a tiger by the tail in Miss Martha, just drink-joking with people to keep from asking them if they remembered the game we beat Wynne, crap that only the quarterback would want to recall, and Claude the quarterback, useless. And ending with me realizing I had pissed away half my life with Rita.

Ruby stood in a different corner, Bubba at her elbow in a blue seersucker suit and red bow tie patiently making chitchat with these people he knew from doing business in the store. He looked so far above them, not only in age but class. All these years I'd been calling him Pluto in my heart, Disney doggy Pluto because of his large baggy eyes. Then, when one of my kids had a special report, I read her myth book and saw there was another Pluto, King of the Underworld, and damned if he didn't grab a young girl and take her off to live with him. And funny thing, the girl stayed with him, half of every year if I remember right. It came to me Ruby has lived more than half her life with him by choice, not mourning, not grieving to be with me. She could have sat up on that barstool in New Orleans and let me dust the sugar off her chin. She could have kissed me full in public. She could have left Bubba and married me, dusting our own two lives with sugar and sweetness.

Just then, she bent down and kissed his shiny head as if she knew I was watching. Pluto, I suddenly remembered, he was a goddamned *king*, not just someone running around chasing maidens and dragging them off to the Underworld.

I got good and drunk. Seeing Ruby and Rita like two points in a triangle and me the third, or Ruby and Bubba and me the third, or me not in any construction at all, just peripheral, as Rita never looked my way even once, called it leaving me to my own devices, and wasn't it *my* reunion and I should have appreciated her tact.

"Tact, what is *that* supposed to mean?" I demanded, but she just pursed her lips like she'd bit a lemon.

"I know what I know," she said, "and if I didn't, don't think there aren't certain people to tell me." The kind of loaded remark I'd have been a fool to answer, and even drunk as I was, I wasn't that far gone.

I ought to be thankful we never were at any other gatherings with Ruby and Bubba. Didn't do anybody any good near as I can tell. Bubba never appeared ruffled. That was a gift, his equanimity, but now it does him no good at all. That party was years ago, we didn't even think about going to the next one. By then, Rita and I, we barely went any place at all if we could help it, not together, that is. Only sugar in my life those pink packets in a bowl on the breakfast table, Sugar Twin.

But Bubba's dead and to be buried tomorrow, and Rita and I will go together to the funeral. After that, I will leave her to her own devices. She can go live with Mary Beth in Memphis if she wants. She can have the house. But this terrible feeling of waiting for something to happen, I won't have to live with it another day. Ruby is free now after all these years. I can't have misjudged that girl. I can see her sitting on that stool in New Orleans, that dust of sugar on her darling chin, her palm in mine, her long life line.

I can see us now.

Adaptation

Frank scarcely leaves his apartment these days. He used to whistle "Oh, Susannah" whenever he saw me in the laundry room or the carport, but now he stays home with his cat, Allstate, he doesn't whistle, and I am having a time living up to my name.

"That will be from Ruby," Frank said as I tore the wrapping off a Jack Daniel's carton that had been sitting in his apartment all afternoon. Those boxes are put together with brass staples; you almost need a crowbar to pry one apart, and he hadn't the strength to attack it. After removing quantities of wadded-up *Commercial Appeals* from Memphis, I pulled out a vase of astonishing color. At the bottom it glowed gilt, and then modulated into smoky green. Just where the vase widened like a woman's hips, it burst into a profusion of roses, pink, magenta, red.

I ran a finger over the gold bumps. "How can you tell who it's from?" Living next door to Frank for three years, I knew a fair amount about his Aunt Ruby in Arkansas, but I saw no label on the box— nothing, save a certain exuberance in the design, to signal Frank's resolute assurance.

"First, the Jack Daniel's, second, the vase. She sends one to all the nieces and nephews when they get married. I suppose she thinks we're getting married, too, or else why would she send it? Maybe, though," his voice grew wavery, "she's just clutching at straws, like me."

Frank tires easily. The AZT, although he'd had high hopes for it, doesn't seem to help in the long run. I am practically living here since his partner, Henry, died six months ago. Frank's not wild about my boyfriend, Sam, but at least they get along.

"*Married*? Us?" What he'd said just sank in.

"I told Ruby not to worry about me, that I was practically living with a nurse. Dietician—big deal, it's like a nurse."

"From practically living with to being married is a big leap."

"Not for Ruby. She's a leaper."

My apartment is on the best side of the building, overlooking the bay and part of the city. You can see clear down to Candlestick Park if you stand on the balcony. Frank's looks into the stone hill on which the apartment building hangs for dear life, a bleak aspect even on a good day.

I have grown used to the way Frank looks, but still, when I knock on his door after work, it's a shock to see him. It's as if something has fallen away during the afternoon, some essential part, one day a bit of cheek, another a strand of arm, as if Frank, wandering from his bedroom to the front room, has sheared off part of himself while walking through the hall.

"Whittled down" is what Sam says. Sam's a cab-inetmaker who works down in San Bruno, and his vocabulary is like that. "Trim," he'll say, admiring me in a new outfit.

Whittled it is for Frank, pared to the essentials. Sam has modified Frank's apartment, installing a handrail for his bathroom, a banister for the entry-way steps.

Stuffing the newspaper back into the Jack Daniel's carton, I found an envelope among the wadding. I held it out to Frank, remembering when I first moved in here. My mom had sent me a greeting card of a woman hanging onto the legs of a flying goose with a huge clock on its back. The card said

"Time flies, whether you're having fun or not." My mom has an eye for cards, never sends sappy. Anyway, I had it on the mantel over the fake fireplace, quite visible that first evening Frank stopped by with a bottle of wine.

"That is *wonderful*," he said, bold as brass picking it up to see who had sent it. "Your mom? Your own mom sent this?"

"Special," I answered. "A congenital optimist, but both eyes open," I told him. "Not a blinker."

"Ruby is like that, my aunt. She's more like my mother than my own mother," he said, and then looked embarrassed.

"What does she do?"

"Used to work in her husband's store, but they sold it before he died. He was Jewish. She was a manicurist before she married him."

"Did she convert?" My sister Mary had married a Jew, and she was considering conversion. She has told me she could give up Christianity, but she isn't sure about taking on *any* religion. I can't imagine my sister becoming religious, let alone Jewish with a name like Mary, but people will do a lot if they love somebody. I asked again. "Did Ruby convert?"

"Naw," Frank drawled, grinning. "She was always a manicurist."

He saw my wine glasses hanging from brackets beneath the cupboard. "You want to crack open that bottle or you want to save it for your junior prom?"

"Oh," I said, startled. "Of course, let me just find where I put the opener."

Frank pulled a Swiss Army knife from the pocket of his jeans. "Not to worry. This baby can do anything. Adapts to a thousand needs." He flipped its various blades, opening and clicking them back into place, ending with a corkscrew sticking out ready for the wine. "I'm a regular Boy Scout."

Of course he was. It didn't take me five minutes to figure that out. He was fun. He still is, only it is getting harder. The medicine depresses him too.

I make custards, dishes that are easy to digest, but he hasn't any appetite. Probably feeds them to Allstate after I leave. There was a time a couple of years ago when Sam and I were having problems, and I was miserable. Frank made a point of taking me out to a movie or to dinner at least once a week. We'd eat Hunan in the Haight or we'd hit one of the Italian places over on 24th Street, one that went heavy on the garlic. These days he hardly eats a thing.

Now, of course, the vase is lying on the rug, and he's sitting there fiddling with the envelope.

His name is scrawled all over it, and up in the corner where a stamp might go, someone has drawn a heart with little wings coming out on each side. I'm staring at this vase and trying not to laugh or cry at his having written Ruby we were practically married. Now what's on his mind is a kind of defiance, going out in style, not being a burden to his relatives. Back home for a while last year when his uncle died, it was a disaster.

"Mama now," he laughed bitterly describing it, "is like a vulture. Just peers at you, running her tongue over her lips all the time, stitching her needlepoint, waiting for you to die or something.

"Ruby had a ton of paperwork, things Bubba left for her to tend, some property they had, just normal stuff a person has to face when a husband dies. Still, she took it into her head that I should stay home there in Arkansas, and she called up an old friend of hers to get him to put me to work in his insurance company. Ruby knew I worked for one out here, so as far as she was concerned, that was that.

"Well, the boss, John Clay Ferris, turned out he and Ruby had been," Frank smiled a knowing smile, "*good friends*, they told me, for years, and there wasn't anything he wouldn't do for her. His wife had just left him, purged about a month's worth of billing from their computer. I knew the program, so I went to work. There was plenty to do. He was friendly, but everybody else in the place gave me a wide berth. They installed a new coffee maker and Styrofoam cups, taking away the mugs everybody used before, like they were afraid I might contaminate them if I used someone's."

"Maybe the old coffee maker belonged to the guy's wife and she took it with her when she left," I said.

"Give me a break. Even paranoids have enemies. It was very uncomfortable. Nobody talked to me, not really. Oh, 'mornin',' and 'how y'all,' banter but never conversation. Standing way around across my desk, never coming anything like close. I couldn't have stayed. Besides cold, it was weird."

"What do you mean?"

"Well, every once in a while I'd get this feeling someone was staring at me, and I'd look up and there he'd be, kind of teary-eyed, this Mr. Ferris, shaking his head, but then when I'd look up, he'd look away. Now, Susannah, I am *used* to men looking at me, but this was different. I thought he must know about my being sick. Finally I asked him."

"You favor your aunt," he told me, blinking. "She never had kids. But if she did, if she'd married someone else and she'd had children, why I expect they would have looked something like you."

"Definitely weird," I agreed.

We never did figure out what that was all about, and this past year, we've had a lot more to think about than Arkansas. I can see, watching Frank hesitate to open the envelope, that he's nervous even thinking about home. What Ruby might write to him, even if it's kind. Poor baby, it's as if he's been thrown into one of those vats they use to strip furniture. Frank put down the envelope and opened the lower cabinet where he keeps the booze. He pulled out a bottle and poured a drink, cocking his head in a gesture that asked if I wanted one too. I did.

Allstate appeared on the balcony that ran around the apartment, and she rubbed against the glass begging to be let in. Frank and I sprawled there over our bourbon watching the wind ruffle Allstate's coat and the glass compress the part of her that was flat against the window.

"You really can't go home again," he said. "Or have it come home to you, not like this."

"Of course you can," I said. I saw his face splinter and recompose itself but lose something in the composition. "But you don't have to," I added, getting up and opening the window to let the cat in. She made straight for Frank's legs.

"Allstate, Sam, and I, well, we're here, honey."

Which is true, although Sam is working on a big job down in Silicon Valley for a computer millionaire, building a six-thousand-square-foot house with no guest room. Sometimes Sam stays overnight to avoid the commute now that the place has electricity and the windows are in. He's talked so much about it, how it looks out over a series of hills covered just now with lupine and poppies. We plan to take Frank for a ride to see it before the flowers fade, one of these days when he's feeling stronger.

I don't know though. Frank and I are sitting here staring at this vase, so damned ugly it's unbelievable. Of the Less Is More school, I like a single rose in a crystal vase. Frank, on the other hand, is forever jamming peonies, roses, even honeysuckle scavenged from a fence up the hill, everything he finds, into a round bowl on his dining table. What can you do? His apartment has the same dinky mantel over the fake fireplace that mine has. Maybe four feet long. And on it, he has a parade of onyx elephants, an assortment of tiny baskets woven of pine needles, seashells from a trip he and Henry took to Mexico, and a tall black art deco vase with peacock feathers at the end. In every socket of his apartment, night-lights hide behind scallop shells. You walk into that apartment at night, as I did to feed his cat when he was in the hospital, and it looks like the electric parade at Disneyland.

I teased him about those lights once. "I can't stand the dark," he said. Now I don't tease. We don't talk about the dark.

Frank said, "I hope you understand about my writing Ruby we were getting married. I don't want to burden anyone." I nod, and as he opens the envelope, a package of Dentyne gum falls out. He holds up the card and reads what his aunt has written: "Plum out of lamps here—you'll have to make do with a vase."

"Ruby used to have lamps with roses on them in her guest room. When I was little, when I spent the night at her house, she always left one on for me."

So we're staring at this vase. He is considering it, running his fingers over its length. Suddenly, though, he holds it high against the light, inspects the base.

"Sturdy," he says. He smiles and brightens visibly before my eyes. He picks the Dentyne up from the floor and peels off two pieces, one for each of us. Then he takes up the lamp again.

"I could take this down to Cliff's," he says. Cliff is dead, but it's still the best hardware store in town, next to the Castro Theatre. Frank points to the Chinese wedding basket by his couch.

"Cliff's grandson cut me a piece of glass just the right size to turn that basket into an end table. We could turn this vase into a lamp. Sam could make a wooden base for it, if he has time; we could wire it right up."

I am amazed. He sounds like he used to sound before he got sick. He sounds, I think darkly, like Mickey Rooney urging his gang to put on a show. "Hell," he continues excitedly, "you can make just about anything into a lamp, a bubble gum machine, a piggy bank—Jesus, Susannah, you've seen! You can make a lamp out of anything."

He lifts it up to the light again, then cradles it as if he's holding a banjo on his knees. He makes a strumming gesture, and I imagine he may whistle "Oh, Susannah," but he doesn't. This giddiness, bravura, is it his medication? The way an Eagle Scout thinks *Be prepared* as if there's a merit badge in dying well? That was what all the old movies were about, but this is the eighties. If he's Mickey Rooney and Audie Murphy all rolled into one, who am I? Judy Garland, Jennifer Jones? I'm Susannah; I *want* to cry for him.

"It practically glows already," Frank says.

Thinking he's talking about her, Allstate stretches and thrusts out her chin, then as I reach to pet her, leaps suddenly onto a chair. The cat almost knocks the vase out of Frank's hands, but he holds on, one pale hand catching the knobby gilt base, the other grasping at the place where the roses bloom.

Wild Goose Chase

At nine o'clock Ruby heard Beatrice walking down the sidewalk and imagined her picking up the morning paper, frowning at curtains still drawn. She wouldn't like what she didn't see through the window: Ruby, sitting over coffee. Ruby lay in bed and reached for the tumbler of bourbon on her nightstand as she heard Bea fumbling now with the door to the back porch, her purse scratching against the screen.

A storage room with an extra refrigerator and a table for garden things, the back porch had been neat when Bea went home Friday. Now the table was a mess, dirt spilled from a bag of potting soil, scissors and a trowel left in the dirt. Ruby took a deep swallow of bourbon. She had meant to clean that up before Bea came in this morning, but the weekend had fairly flown away. Where had it gone?

"Uhn, uhnn," she heard Beatrice mutter, knew she was looking at the Jack Daniel's carton torn open with two bottles gone, the other four upright in their narrow corrugated slots. Ruby set the glass down and pulled the covers up over her head so as not to hear Bea's clucks of dismay as she walked in on the pile of dishes in the sink, plates ribbed with fish bones, and a bowl Ruby had dipped the fish in, cornmeal, salt, pepper spilled on the counter.

Beatrice swore, Ruby heard it, at the cast iron skillet on the stove filmed with congealed Crisco. She heard faucets running, the tea kettle clatter as it was set to boil, then Bea as she began to address the dishes, loud, for Ruby's benefit.

"Go ahead, make some racket. Summon the dead if you think you can." The tea kettle whistled. "You too," she told it. "All the noise in the world not going to bring Mr. Bubba back. Question is, can we get a rise out of Miz Ruby or do she be too far gone this morning?"

"I hear you," Ruby called. "You trying to wake the dead?"

"Just checking."

Ruby came slowly to the kitchen door clutching a silk paisley robe. Her hair hung around her shoulders. She still tinted it auburn although it was more subdued than it had been in her youth. Her skin was freckled now as much by age as sun, her body thicker but still erect.

"I feel a year older than God this morning."

Bea looked up from drying the skillet. "Come nigh to looking like it, you forgive me saying so."

"I don't remember when I fell asleep. Made some catfish, but I got lonesome, poured myself a drink, just one."

"Just one when?"

"Then."

"What those bottles?"

"You sound like Martha Nell," Ruby said, pushing her hair back from her face. "Make us some coffee, please."

Beatrice set a place at the breakfast table for Ruby, then stood leaning against the wall while she drank her own coffee.

"Looks like you had a party here only nobody came. You got to get ahold of yourself. Mister Bubba been dead and gone two years. You got to stop wearing his robe. It don't even have his scent no more, and it never fit you. It's too narrow through the shoulders. Look there—you split a seam." She pointed and frowned. "You got lovely robes yourself. Three, four of them, not counting that ostrich feather thing Mr. Ferris done had delivered here. Not that you want to wear that in the morning," she finished, smiling broadly. "Still, why you be wearing this old thing? You can't bring him back that way."

Ruby set her coffee cup carefully in its saucer. Her hand shook. She blinked and then tried to focus on the hedge beyond her window where small pink and white floral trumpets of deutzia provided safe refuge for the bumblebees. Her teeth felt fuzzy. She wished for some place to crawl into and hide, some place sweet and deep like the inside of a flower. She squinted, rubbed her forehead, then felt her shoulder.

"Falling apart at the seams, that's what you're saying?"

"No disrespect intended, but somebody has to tell you. Who else is there?" Bea smoothed her hands on her apron. "I been working for you forty years. Known you afore that from Booker Suggs, you remember?"

"Booker Suggs?" Ruby frowned. "I'm sure I should. I'm not myself this morning."

"Booker my cousin. Used to live downcountry near the place your daddy worked."

Ruby smiled. "A thousand years ago. A thousand and one. Now I remember. How is he? He isn't dead, is he?"

"Booker the foreman out to Mr. Bridgeford's farm all these years. Now he's retired; gone on the disability. Doing real fine. Doing a little gardenin' for cash, know what I mean?"

"Collecting his social security." Ruby's eyes creased.

"Was Booker done told me about you, said you were a good woman. That's why I come to work for you. You forget that?"

"Been so long, Bea, don't be cross. I'm going to hell in a handbasket. Don't tell him."

"He can see for hisself," Bea said, "if you let him come out to do your garden. The garden club ladies coming here next week and more weeds than you can shake a stick at. Dahlias need staking. A little help wouldn't hurt you. Nor cutting back on your other foolishness."

Ruby picked at the sleeve of Bubba's old robe. Bea was not only her housekeeper but her friend of long standing who stood as mother to her (although Bea was several years younger) and as sister (although not nearly so critical as Martha Nell). It was a reciprocal relationship, complicated.

Hadn't she, although it troubled her to misplace Booker Suggs like that, hadn't she helped Bea with her divorce when she wanted to dump Levester Walker, had a Rotary friend of Bubba's do the legal work for Bea? And didn't she sit every afternoon when she was home chatting and listening to stories about Bea's church ladies? But it was bothersome the way Bea bossed her, like this business with the robe. Whose was it anyway?

"Yes," she said absently, "let Booker Suggs come along. He can't be any stiffer than I am when it comes to bending over a flower bed." She pushed her coffee cup fretfully away and retreated to her bedroom where she drank the last of the bourbon in her glass, then looked at Bubba's shirts hanging in his closet. She fingered one softly as she did each morning before going about her business. Touching his shirt was like talking to him.

"Mister Bubba *gone*. How long you going to leave them shirts be? Clothes should've been out of here the first month."

Ruby spun around. "I didn't hear you."

"Head like you wearing this morning, wonder you hear the Lord should He call you." Bea wrinkled her face in distaste at the sight of the bottle on Ruby's nightstand.

"Give those clothes to the church. Make some use of them. So many people could be using them." She paused. "Else maybe make something out of them shirts." She looked to see how Ruby was taking this.

"Make something? Do what?"

"You could make a quilt. We could do it together. I show you how, the way my momma done taught me." Bea smiled. "'Course I was little. It was a string quilt, but it learnt me fine. I been quiltin' ever since." She looked at Bubba's shirts as if she could already see them taking shape beneath her fingers. Then she looked again at Ruby and played her best card.

"A nice cover for your bed, keep you warm, little pieces of Mister Bubba's shirts all shaped up for you to wake up every morning, comfort." She hesitated. Ruby was standing very still, her head inclined slightly as if she wanted not to miss a word. "Comfort not out of that bottle, comfort not giving you these headaches in the morning."

Ruby looked down at Beatrice's head, which ducked now in apprehension lest she had overstepped herself. Bea's fine hair was white as a cotton boll, puffing around her lined forehead. Tiny gold ear rings dangled from her ears, whimsical piglets Ruby and Bubba had brought her from one of their journeys out of Arkansas, years ago. Then Bea looked up. Ruby smiled, Bubba's shirts like a curtain behind her, the way he himself had always been, backing her up no matter how far out beyond the boundaries she went. Unconsciously she rubbed her hands, feeling her rings; they slipped a little.

"I have hardly stitched more than a button in my life except to hem."

"A quilt," Bea repeated, rubbing her own hands, one thumb massaging the other, "you could piece a quilt, Miz Ruby. This is good cotton, the best. It would quilt up fine."

"I don't have the patience. All those stitches."

"My church group do the quilting part after you do the piecing." Beatrice smiled. "I help you. You never too old to learn. Do you good."

"I don't need any do-goodin', thank you very much," Ruby said stiffly. But Bea stood her ground, folded her strong arms in front of her and looked steadily at Ruby.

"You gonna make it. You been making it, but I be putting out the empty liquor bottles every week now. I be washing up your fancies. I know you inside out and backwards. You got too much time on your hands."

"Nonsense," Ruby said faintly.

"I got faith in the Lord. He giving you strength and courage to keep on. But He ain't gon' step down here and hand you this one. You gon' have to get up and go get it." Then Bea left the room.

Over drinks later that week, Ruby's sister Martha Nell surprised her by agreeing with Beatrice.

"It's a generous offer. Those women at Third Baptist do the finest quilting for miles. You would have a treasure. I have a book of patterns," she added. "I bought it because it has some terrific flowers for embroidery. You'll love it. You can pick out something easy."

"It could be something hard," Ruby said. "I'm not incompetent. Besides, I have Beatrice to help me and lots of time. I have even more time now I've hired Bea's cousin to help me in the garden. He is good with my roses, knows what to do. I have more time than I know what to do with . . ."

Since Bubba's death, Ruby had become very careful of time. Before, it had flowed steadily with few interruptions, and she had taken little notice of it. But for the past two years, she noticed who was punctual and who late, and she found herself waking at exactly the same moment every morning. This frightened her, and mornings when she'd managed to sleep deeper, later, she felt she had beat some clock that ticked despite her own will.

Once awake though, she pigeonholed her friends with respect to time as she had never done all the years of her married life. Martha Nell was always late. The women's garden club meetings never began later than five minutes past the hour for which they were called. The beauty parlor where she had her hair touched up always ran late, but then if she was late herself, the operator would sure as shootin' be standing there with a towel draped over her arm, stopping just short of toe-tapping to chastise her. John Clay Ferris was punctual to a fault, and always had been.

It was impossible to forget what he had been like at sixteen or twenty-six, even at thirty-five when she'd thought to have broken with him for good. He was like a metronome against her life with Bubba. He'd been there measuring even when, with great effort, she'd tried to put him out of mind to concentrate completely on her marriage. For years she had nodded politely whenever their paths crossed, but she had put a stop to their desperate meetings all over Arkansas and devoted herself to Bubba. Then when her husband died, John Clay had promptly divorced his wife and presented himself again at her door.

Wasn't life something else? All the clocks ticking as if they kept the same time and nobody in step even with the people they'd known longest and best? She had really believed John Clay had got her out of his system when all that time he was, to hear him tell it, just *waiting* until Bubba died. Twenty-five years of waiting, not counting the twenty before that when they'd sneaked out together.

Ruby sat looking at Martha Nell, her long fingers wrapped around a glass as her sister riffled through pages of a pattern book for a particular pattern she wanted Ruby to consider. She glanced over at Frank's picture on the end table, thought of the way John Clay had given her nephew a job right after Bubba died, those months she and Martha Nell had believed Frank should stay in Arkansas, not return to San Francisco. And John Clay steady as the minute hand, making a place for him in his own insurance company, Frank clearly weak but still able to work.

She pictured the two of them in the office Uptown, John Clay in his brown suit at one desk near the window, Frank in a khaki suit which hung too loosely, sitting at a computer. Frank had worn plaid shirts all the time, thinking they filled him out. John Clay had become so much a respectable town fixture he only wore white shirts, and it was with difficulty that Ruby remembered him at Frank's age, far more flamboyant, less cautious.

Truth to tell, when she thought of John Clay young, she couldn't remember him in anything more substantial than a T-shirt, and that was stretching some. She smiled.

If she made this quilt, she would use Bubba's shirts, only Bubba's shirts, but she *would* have liked to put in something of Frank's and something of John Clay's, only she knew Martha Nell had not brought any of Frank's clothes home from San Francisco after his funeral. She hardly knew how she'd sneak one of John Clay's shirts past Beatrice's eagle eye. Bea knew every garment in that closet from years of washing and ironing. She set the notion aside.

"Here now," Martha Nell said triumphantly, "just look at this one." The pattern showed a circle of iris and tulips in a basket. A long border of ribbons floated from the basket's base.

"I have enough flowers with the garden club," Ruby said taking the book. Baskets, cake plates, trees of life, flower after appliquéd flower, and then, there it was, a series of triangles flying across a page. She could see Bubba's shirts, or pieces of them, taking flight across her bed, and she slid her glasses down her nose to see what this pattern was called. She laughed out loud.

"What's so gol-durned funny?" Martha Nell asked suspiciously.

"Wild Goose Chase," Ruby said. "Now isn't that the truth? Isn't that just the pattern we will do, Beatrice and me?"

"Fitting," Martha Nell agreed. "Don't know why I didn't think of it myself. That or Robbing Peter to Pay Paul."

It proved to be a pattern Beatrice liked. It turned out that Booker Suggs himself could cut material. He had worked several afternoons in Ruby's garden, shy for about ten seconds, then happy to have his hands back in dirt. Equally pleased to step into the kitchen for iced tea and curious about the quilt project that was taking over the dining room.

Booker, Beatrice, and Ruby stood around Ruby's dining table, on which Bea had placed the table pads and spread out two of Bubba's shirts. Sleeves removed, the torsos bore scarcely any resemblance to Bubba's shape.

"Sit down, Booker, don't just stand there," Bea directed, as she took a chair herself. Ruby hung back watching while Bea set the template of a triangle again and again down the length of cotton, penciling around it then handing the section across to Booker for cutting.

"This part requires a steady hand," Booker told Ruby, "an' I was used to help my Ethel. Me and her, we got along like two fingers on one hand."

Ruby stiffened. Had Beatrice told Booker about her drinking, her wobblies? Stealthily she extended one of her own hands, just near her side where she could regard its steadiness or lack of balance. She had tried to cut back, adding more water, less bourbon, since Beatrice had taken her to task. Her hand was shaky; she couldn't deny it.

She looked over at Booker, but he was bent over cutting carefully, and she tried to remember the way he looked trudging along the side of the road to the colored school while she rode past in the bus restricted then to white students. But now Booker was bent even when he was standing straight, his hair gray, and he bore absolutely no resemblance to any picture she could conjure up. He looked much older than John Clay or herself although they were all within a year or so of one another. She sighed.

That clock, it must have been running double time for Booker and Beatrice. Ruby looked across at Bea, whose lip was stuck out in concentration, and over Bea's head in the beveled glass of her own sideboard, she saw herself standing there, no spring chicken. Life had not dealt unkindly with her, clocks telling her time to help Bubba on Saturdays, time to go to Memphis for shopping with Martha Nell, time to quit cheating on Bubba with John Clay, time on her hands when she and Bubba had been unable to have children. All that time slipping through her fingers as easily as this cotton slipped away out of a man's shape and into triangles beneath the cousins' scissors. Although enveloped in dismay for the new shape of things, she realized that now the clock was saying it was time to shape up.

She squinted over at herself, saw her jaw slack, and her chin developing a twin. Her eyes, which had always sparkled, seemed dull. What did John Clay see in her now? She was a mess. Even from here she could discern in her cheeks an unattractive blush. Whenever she saw someone with similar markings she always thought "drunk." Oh, God, this was not how she thought she looked at all, not how she was, but wasn't she tottering here eyeing the decanter while Beatrice and Booker Suggs cut up Bubba's shirts for her ultimate comfort? Almost a bystander in her own life?

"I want to try some cutting there myself," she said in such a voice that Booker jumped and Bea caught up the fabric she was spreading and held it against her chest.

"Course you do," said Bea motioning to Booker. "Booker, see do those sprinklers need resetting in the garden, and Miz Ruby and I, we do a bit together."

Oh—patronized by her own help. She could hardly stand it, but Bea sat her down and handed over the template.

"I get carried away," Bea said quietly. "Get so excited beginning a quilt—been too long since I have pieced one. And having Booker here—his wife Ethel, dead now, but she was a fine woman." Bea sighed. "Just tracing and cutting with Booker put me in mind of old times. I plain forgot myself. This is our project, yours and mine. We make Booker stay in the garden."

Ruby shook her head. "I want to cut me some of this cotton," she said, seizing the scissors. Energetically she cut, but when she held the piece up, it was more trapezoid than triangle. She set it down. "I have ruined it."

"Don't nobody do things perfect the first time," said Bea. "Booker been cutting pieces for his Ethel for years. I been doing this since I was a child. We give you something else to practice on and then we start again. Just you and me."

"No," Ruby said, "There will be plenty of work for all of us. I'm not sure I'm really up for this, Bea." She looked at the cotton, saw how wide of the mark she had cut. It seemed not like a triangle but a mockery of the idea. She caught her breath. She looked over at the bourbon on the sideboard. "God damn it to hell."

"Ain't nothing can't be fixed," said Bea.

John Clay arrived that evening to take Ruby to a movie. She greeted him at the door with scissors in her hand.

"I'm not quite ready. Pour yourself a drink. I'll just put these away. I won't be a minute."

"What is this?" he asked, surveying her dining table.

"Bea is making a project out of me." Ruby laughed a little self-consciously, taking the drink John Clay had mixed for her, looking down at Bubba's shirts on the table.

"You don't have enough dustcloths? Looks like you're cutting good shirts for nothing. Somebody could wear those. Collars are wide, but there's folks that wouldn't care a whit. A shame to cut them up like this." John Clay frowned and took a deep drink.

"We are making a quilt," Ruby said.

"*We?*"

"Beatrice, Booker Suggs, and me."

"Oh, that's fine. That's wonderful. What's got into you?"

"Time," she said. "Too much time on my hands."

"Marry me," he said, for perhaps the tenth time.

"Come on now, we don't want to miss the movie." Ruby took his glass and set it next to hers. She was surprised to see that both were empty; it could not have been ten minutes since he'd arrived.

Weeks went by. Every Wednesday, Booker's day to help Ruby in the garden, turned into a miniature quilting bee around the dining table, and slowly the pattern began to emerge. Blocks began to fit together like a puzzle, and Ruby saw promise in the bits of cloth she put together on her own.

"Good," Bea always told her, never diminishing her labor by criticism. "Better," she would then say, taking the seam ripper and tearing apart a block where the juxtaposition of colors was not to her liking, "if you put this checked gingham over here, and keep the stripe next to the solid blue, that fine chambray," Bea sighed, "Lord, wasn't that just Mr. Bubba's very favorite shirt of all?" She smoothed the cloth fondly, as if remembering Bubba's passion for clean starched shirts and the years she had laundered and ironed them.

One day she came into Ruby's house with a plastic bag of fabric, strings of red cloth sewn together in irregular strips. Some pieces were broadcloth, some flannel.

"These hold the blocks together," she told Ruby. "Red, it stands out fine and far. Nothing holds a quilt together like a good red." Patiently, Bea showed Ruby how to combine the blocks, using the red bands to anchor the whole.

"Just look how it shimmies." Ruby clapped her hands. Bea and Ruby moved the pieces spread out on the dining table around together as if playing solitaire, only together. Bea pointed to the triangles flying up and down the borders with Bubba's shirts in place. "These are the wild geese," she said. "They fly. This be one movin' quilt top." She laughed. "My church ladies will be plenty surprised. I always told them you something else."

Ruby and Booker spoke less formally, almost as if they were old friends. He was kind, she told her sister, and even in her own dining room she felt herself becoming someone else. At five o'clock, when Bea and Booker left, Ruby stayed at the dining table moving bits of fabric around. The decanter of bourbon stood on the sideboard behind her.

One evening, Martha Nell came over to inspect the project. Ruby watched as her sister circled the table, picking up a block for close inspection, setting it back down. Rarely did Ruby care for anyone's good opinion, but now she was anxious that Martha Nell approve. The idea of including something of her nephew's and something of John Clay's had continued to run through Ruby's mind like a basting stitch, loose but steady. She thought of the way John Clay had stood looking down at Bubba's shirts. Although she didn't want to marry again, she had read in his face the desire for some scrap of their own history to be verified. Marriage was his idea, that knot, but she thought the quilt would be easier to live with. Frank's was another life that needed tacking down.

"Anyone ask me who made this Wild Goose Chase," she began, "I am going to tell them, me and my sewing circle, yes I am. We're getting to be like three fingers on one hand."

"It's one hell of a project." Martha Nell fingered one of the blocks.

Tentatively Ruby said, "It's going to be a big quilt. I maybe could make it big enough for *all* the men in my life." She looked at Martha Nell, but her sister simply laid the block back on the table without saying anything.

"Do you happen to have anything of Frank's I could use? I was thinking maybe those old Boy Scout badges on his Eagle Scout sash. We could snip them off if you wouldn't mind."

"You're using shirts. His badges would be out of place."

"He was such a darlin'," Ruby said. "If I'd had kids of my own, I'd stitch in every bit of what I had left from when they were little. Every living thing I could lay my hands on. This is for comfort, this quilt. It's got to be *full*."

"You think you'd have things, scraps and whatnot. Truth is, it disappears," sighed Martha Nell. "Time was, my whole house was a clutter of Frank's junk. I can't be sentimental about it. I hated it. Everywhere I looked, model airplane glue stuck on the kitchen counter or tennis rackets falling off shelves. I thought I'd never see the end of it. Then before I knew it," she looked away from Ruby and out the window, "gone. Empty. A place for everything, and everything in its place. It's no comfort, I can tell you that."

Ruby looked down and picked up a bit of fabric. Martha Nell went on. "It's going to take you a long time to make this quilt. Don't get carried away and ruin the pattern."

Ruby sniffed. "Shoot, Martha Nell, you telling me to worry about a *pattern*? Far as I can see, a pattern's only good as a starting point. You got to make it up as you go along."

Martha Nell nodded. "Frank would like that, I know he would." Martha Nell picked up one of the strips of red Beatrice had brought in. Ruby saw it suddenly as Martha Nell must see with her eyes for perfection.

"You do beautiful embroidery," she said, "every little thread in place, but my quilt is going to be different. Yes, I want patches from Frank's scouting. Want the tassel from his drum major's hat you got tucked away on a shelf. Bits and snips, whatever you have."

She took a deep breath and plunged on. "I am fixing to tuck in something of John Clay too. Don't look at me like that. I have decided. This quilt is going to have a piece of all the men in my life." Ruby expected Martha Nell to say something ugly, but Martha Nell just grinned.

"This would tickle Frank to death. You show me what you want to do, maybe I can figure out a place to appliqué those Scout patches. Maybe more than two or three." Now she hesitated herself. "I am good at appliqué. I'd be pleased to sew them on for you. Could be we could place them on those red strips, where they'll intersect to connect the blocks. I reckon that's how Beatrice is planning to set this up."

"I need all the help I can get. Making a quilt isn't like anything else I've ever done." Ruby gestured toward the living room, and they sat down, leaving blocks of fabric scattered on the dining table. Leaving the sideboard with its decanters untouched.

"I've noticed," said Martha Nell, "you are doing things differently. Or not doing them."

Ruby leaned back against her chair and looked over at her sister. Cautiously she said, "Tried to quit cold turkey. Bad idea. I was out in the garden one morning before it got too hot, Booker Suggs helping stake my dahlias. I saw somebody in the row there out the corner of my eye. At first I thought it was Booker, but when I looked up, it was Frank."

"Are you off your rocker?"

"I wouldn't make this up. I swear to God, Martha Nell, he was there. He was about ten, wearing a cowboy hat tied around his neck, and those shorts that flapped around his thin little legs, cowboy boots too. He was crying.

"'What's the matter, baby?' I asked him.

"'Big boys chased me home, called me sissy.'

"I told him to run on home and tell you, but he cried harder."

Now Ruby stopped as if she'd thought better of things, but Martha Nell said crossly, "Go on, then. What happened next? What'd he say?"

"'I did,' he said. 'Mama told me she'd whup me herself if I didn't fight back. I can't go out and I can't go home, so I came here.'

"'Your mama just tryin' to make a little man of you,' I told him. 'Don't you see you have to stand up to those bullies else they'll chase you the rest of your life?'

"Then Booker looked over from his row of dahlias tsk-tsking to beat the band. My hands were shaking so I could hardly hold my hoe. 'You speaking to me?' he asked. And I realized I was talking out loud, Martha Nell, having a . . . what you call it? A hallucination. I mean I *saw* Frank, no bigger than my tallest dahlia, the orange one. So much for cold turkey. I went straight in and poured myself a drink. Told Booker I'd had too much sun."

Martha Nell wiped her eyes.

"I poured it half out and filled it with Coke the way I used to do around Maude," Ruby offered.

"And then?"

"I drank it. But every day, I've been drinking half and then after a week, half of that, more Coke." She held out her hand. "Look. Shaking but not rattling. I am cutting *way* back; see can I catch hold of myself. Whenever I get nervous, I take up the quilt, piece some more of those triangles together. It steadies me, all those bits of Bubba's shirts. Tonight I am going to ask John Clay for one of his old shirts. I don't know what I am going to tell Beatrice."

Ruby took a pack of Kleenex from her pocket and handed it silently to Martha Nell. Then she smoothed out the block of quilting she'd brought into the living room. She felt good, like she used to feel before Bubba died, before Frank succumbed.

"This is not any big deal," she said finally. "I am not altogether quitting on bourbon. This quilt is not the Be All and the End All. I was hoping it would be, but I see it's just going to be a comforter. You know how you get hold of a little bit of something and you think you've got the whole thing under control? Getting back on course," she said quietly, "and this here seems as good a place to start as any." Ruby smoothed the block of fabric, traced a lacquered fingernail around some blue chambray. Five triangles, the "geese," appeared to fly over her lap.

Come and Sit
by My Side

Not a good week to miss work, but nobody needed to tell Michelle that people didn't consider convenience when they died. Flying low, clocking ninety, now that she was out of Little Rock, she swerved around a dead possum on the highway and wondered whether her father would show up at Grandma's funeral. Mama sounded more than a little sloshed on the phone. Sloshed and ticked.

"Molly can't come. That damned museum. More important than family," she said. "You'd better get on back if you want to see your grandma before they close the coffin. Do you have anything you can wear to a funeral?"

"Mama!"

At her grandmother's funeral, Michelle wore her darkest dress, a rayon print with a neckline Elizabeth had deemed too scooped, inappropriate. If Molly had been there to calm her, things wouldn't have got so far out of hand over nothing. But Molly, her mother, Elizabeth's, first cousin and best friend, was up to her eyelashes in a major exhibit back in San Francisco: the French consul was hosting the entire diplomatic community the night before their formal opening, and she simply could not leave. Did they understand?

Yes, and no. Michelle did, her mother didn't. *Come and sit by my side if you love me.* By the time Michelle arrived, her mother was steaming. "You said you had something appropriate," she began, as Michelle hung the dress in the closet.

"Mama, it's what I had in Little Rock. I left work twenty minutes after you called. They were very nice about it at the law firm. What do you want from me?"

"Something appropriate. Not a cocktail dress. My God!"

Michelle tried to ignore her, focused on whether her father would show up. He had never gotten along well with his mother-in-law. If ever there was an occasion to miss, this would be it. Harder and harder to count on, he'd not attended Michelle's college graduation, so it was startling, next day, to see him hovering at the rear of the funeral home as if debating whether to offer condolences.

His hair. Whatever had he done to his hair? Gray the last time she'd seen him, it was practically orange, orangutan orange, and shaggy as ever. Michelle was determined to be pleasant, recalling the numerous times her mother had said over the years, "I'm the one with the divorce, not you, not your brother."

Difficult, though, to be exactly happy to see him. It had been a long time since she and Dennis had tried leaving messages on his answering machine. At least he wore a suit, had made some effort to be presentable. When her father finally came forward, he said, "I feel your pain," and walked away. She'd rather he had been anything but ridiculous. Fathers were not supposed to be ridiculous. They were supposed to have dignity, charm, and humor like her grandfather had. How *could* her mother have married someone so different from her own father, so totally weird?

Later that evening, when Molly got away from her museum reception long enough to call to ask how everyone was holding up, Michelle asked her that very question.

"When Elizabeth and I were your age, women tried to marry someone different from their fathers, consciously, since nobody in those days got out of school without studying Freud in Psych 101, and nobody stayed single long enough after graduation to have forgotten it. Now, tell me how your mama's doing."

After being persuaded to speak to Molly, Elizabeth fumed all over again to the others about Michelle's dress, about Molly's absence.

"How *could* she not come for her own aunt's funeral? If it had been Ruby, she'd be here no matter what. Sorry, Ruby, I don't mean to say I think you're going any time soon. I am just rattled, that's all." Then she noted her own surprise at seeing Michelle's father at the service. "That orange hair. God. The man you divorce is *not* the man you married."

Ruby, who'd stayed to help put things away, was working on an iced tea glass filled with bourbon. She winked at Michelle. What nobody said but what Michelle had figured out was that her parents had to get married because of her.

Aunt Ruby had let it slip one time when Michelle was just starting to date. "You be more careful than your mama," she'd said. "You want to finish school." Then she'd tried to make out like she was only joking, had had too much to drink. Everything was a mess that whole time, Frank walking around like a skeleton before he went back to San Francisco to die of AIDS, everyone pretending he was going to be all right, trying to keep from Dennis and Michelle the fact that he was queer, as if they didn't know, and who cared anyway? Lots of people were, not necessarily in their town, but in Memphis.

Once they could drive, all the kids would drive over to the blues clubs, and sometimes they'd detour into neighborhoods where men dressed like women and walked the streets. Never did anything ugly, just looked, trying to figure out who was a man, who wasn't. Frank wasn't like that. He'd been really sweet to both her and her brother those months he was back, had given her his Rolling Stones albums, his Beatles *Abbey Road* and Pink Floyd tapes. He'd given Dennis his red Craftsman tool set, which was still out in Ruby's garage where he used to have a workshop when he was their age. Dennis was in Scouts then, and he was thrilled to have those tools. Frank said he'd give him his Eagle Scout sash too, but Dennis wasn't interested.

Dennis, poor little Dennis. That he was over six feet tall didn't matter—he was still her kid brother. Where was he anyway? As soon as he could get away, right after they'd left the cemetery, he'd got into his truck and driven off.

Michelle wondered if it was better to lose a parent to death rather than to divorce, knowing for a certainty you'd never hear that voice at the end of the phone, spared the continual disappointment of hope in spite of itself. Years now since her parents' marriage ended, and she couldn't help it: once in awhile, in spite of everything, she missed her father. Maybe not really *him*, but the idea of a father. People said things came in threes. This was the second funeral inside of a year. She thought about John Clay, whose funeral had taken place at the beginning of summer. He had always been real nice to Dennis, and to her, too, trying to be something between an uncle and a father. Still, to Michelle he was simply this romantic old guy who'd gone off to fight the war in the South Pacific and returned to find his own true love, Ruby, married to Bubba.

After John Clay's funeral, Michelle had to drive back to school to finish her exams, but she'd returned immediately afterwards to spend a week with Ruby before her summer internship began in Little Rock. Her mother had insisted. "I don't need you to help me with your grandma's stuff. I had me a tag sale after we moved her into Senior House. I need you to help Ruby this week. Please come over around five. We'll take ice cream to Grandma after supper."

Ruby's house was a mess, Ruby not much better, looking like she'd been living in her bathrobe, not even bothering to dress. All day, Ruby went through old photo albums, scrapbooks, drawers. She pulled the cloth off the dining room table and spread pictures on it as if she was playing solitaire. Snapshots slipped around the highly polished surface. Too brittle for shuffling, many were the size of playing cards, sepia and tan, or after a while, black and white, but no color prints. Michelle saw pictures of her mother and Molly, as well as a whole slew of other little kids she'd heard names of, other cousins who lived, as Molly had, in St. Louis, or in Cleveland.

"See here, now," Ruby held one up. "You've heard about your mama's cousin David who was killed in the Munich Olympics when you were a baby? Here he is with your mama, Molly, and Marilee, just a toddler then." She shook her head. "Not much older than you are now when those terrorists murdered him. Killed all his teammates, too. I had a news clipping of that in here, but I don't see it." She rummaged further.

"Look at this ridiculous picture," said Ruby, lifting a Peabody Hotel photograph of Bubba and herself in a younger incarnation. Ruby's dress revealed much of her bosom, a stone marten scarf draped over her shoulders, a cigar jutting out of Bubba's mouth, the table before them littered with champagne bottles, New Year's hats and horns. A gray mat surrounded this photo, *Starlight Room* stamped in gold in the corner.

"You look like a movie star," said Michelle.

"Oh, yeah?" Ruby pointed to another one, in which she held up a mess of fish, taken downriver, to judge from the scenery.

"Yeah, like wow," Michelle insisted, pointing to another one from about the same time, Ruby sitting by the river, silhouetted against the sky, unaware of being photographed.

"Every girl looks good when she's young," Ruby sighed. "Only one chin. Here's one of your mother in the Model T." Every kind of snapshot from the forties, the fifties, and sixties lay semisorted on the table, then not much of anything for a long time. Then Frank, her mother, and Molly, their graduation photos, high school and college, emptiness, as if everyone had gone off and forgotten to write or send anything at all. Frank's funeral notice from ten years ago, just short of his fortieth birthday, Martha Nell's a few years later.

Around and around the table Ruby wandered, talking to herself, moving pictures into some sequence whose significance was lost on Michelle.

"I cannot believe there is not one picture of John Clay from those years. I have our high school year-book." She pulled it out of a bookshelf by the fireplace, opened it. "You see how handsome he was?" Michelle sat next to her on the sofa, turning fragile pages of the old maroon book embossed with a Mustang and 1942. "Who's this other boy with you?"

"My cousin Claude, John Clay's best friend. He died in the war, right next to John Clay on a beach landing, Luzon."

The sofa sagged, enveloped them in faded cabbage roses. The hooked rug beneath their feet needed a good shaking. In front of them, on the coffee table, rings from glasses left years of circles, patterns going nowhere, and Michelle just stared at Claude, an eighteen year old smiling somewhat formally, his light hair raked by a comb. She watched Ruby flip pages until there he was again in the front row center of the football team, helmet resting on his left knee like all the others, the team's quarterback, alive in this picture, looking as if he'd just stopped laughing. She waited for Ruby to say more, but she said nothing.

Finally she turned a page. Another. Set the book down, picked up a small album whose photos were held in place with cornered tabs she'd glued in more than forty years before.

Ruby cleared her throat. "Here's Frank as a baby—holding him, my sister, Martha Nell. They lived in Little Rock during the war. Here's all the cousins down from St. Louis, and the Cleveland cousins too. Here is David. There he is with Marilee, his sister, and your mama. That's your great-granddaddy, Daddy Doc they called him, his Scottie Rip, your grandma and her sister Eva, that was Molly's mama. Molly when she was about two or three." It wasn't easy to follow, Michelle thought, but Ruby knew at a glance which girl was which. The young women who had grown into grandmothers looked to be about her own age in these snapshots. Ruby herself was maybe thirty. Almost fifty years had passed, yet it was clear as yesterday to her.

"Your mama isn't in this one, but here she is, here's both of them, Elizabeth and Molly." Ruby pointed with one of her long nails, and Michelle was surprised to see it chipped. Ruby always took such care of her nails.

"Elizabeth and Molly, and a lifeguard they had such a crush on one summer. I can't remember his name, but they like to run me crazy driving them out to the pool all summer long for lifesaving lessons. It wasn't a far drive."

"What do you mean?" Something in Ruby's voice she hadn't heard before was like the rumble of a bass beneath the melody, curious, necessary in a way she couldn't define except that its presence made it clear that previous comments were thin lines of communication, narrative threads of a sub-text rich in meaning.

"I was caught that summer between desire and desire," Ruby said flatly as if she was speaking about someone she barely acknowledged. "I was never more myself, but close to crazy. I thought I could have everything I wanted, so long as I didn't hurt anybody else. I loved Bubba, really loved him; he made me happy, took good care of me. And he needed me."

She paused. Michelle cocked her head to one side, waiting for Ruby to begin again. "I loved John Clay too. Could not get him out of my system. Summers were the worst, all peach perfumes, petunias, those little sweaty scents, everything ripe. We'd meet up at the icehouse, John Clay and I, until your mother and Molly began to notice him there when we'd stop for ice on our way home from the pool. Then we had to find some other way to plan how we were going to get together, where. We couldn't use the phones; the operators listened in on every conversation."

She shook her head. "It wasn't like it is now. You'd pick up the phone, say 'nine-eight, please,' and the operator would say something like 'Oh, Miz Davidson, they've just gone out. Doc Davidson's back at the office, and Miz Fogg was planning to pick up Miz Maude to go driving at one o'clock.' They listened to everybody, so how could John Clay and I use a phone?

"Used to meet out at Claude's parents' farm. Sometimes we'd drive other places. Once, I've never told this to anyone, I met John Clay in New Orleans, but that was so overwhelming, I left him there and came back by myself, a wink away from leaving Bubba, no good reason but swept away by love. Anybody tells you you can't love but one man at a time, they don't know what they're talking about. I'm here to tell you," she patted Michelle's arm, closed the album. "Love is selfish, you got it, you want it, you want it to last forever like it was, all shiny and shimmery. Bubba and I had got comfortable, the shimmer kind of dimmed, at least for me. It wasn't fair to leave him over that. John Clay was married too. Was I going to break up his family?"

"What did you do? What did you do?" Michelle asked.

"Quit cold turkey, yes siree. Hard, honey? It was living hell. Need against need against need." Ruby clasped her hands, extended her arms in a stretch before her, then abruptly dropped them into her lap.

"I'd pass John Clay in the street, see through the window of his business just across Washington from our store, pretend not to see him looking out for me. Sometimes I'd drive around the back, see was there a parking space there, but we had to leave it free for deliveries, so I'd end up parked out front, and I'd see him. Longing? Stretched tight as the telephone wires, one end of town to the other. Loopy, charged. No place to put that longing. Only time in my whole entire life I wanted time to pass quick, quick, just sense enough to know I had to stop, that a year from then the pain would *have* to be dulled." Ruby cleared her throat. "Maybe a year from now . . ."

Michelle sat not knowing whether to say something or keep still. Ruby spoke as if she was an oracle inside a dark cave, as if she was in a trance.

"*Fish got to swim, birds got to fly, I got to love one man till I die.* Oh, that was me. Your mama and Molly, I took them to see *Show Boat* at the Uptown Cinema. Damned if those little stinkers didn't say I looked like Ava Gardner when she was singing that very song. 'My red hair,' I told them. 'No, your sad eyes,' Molly said. Won't forget if I live to be a hundred, caught out by twelve year olds. Maybe fourteen by then. Bubba, God bless his heart, never said a word, but if those itty-bits could see it, sure he did too."

Pay attention here, Michelle told herself. Her mother never said word one about her love life, though she had a new guy in her life, and he fit in well enough, treated Elizabeth with respect, affection. He had told Dennis they'd go water-skiing at Lake of the Ozarks sometime, and her brother's face had lit up. Didn't they all have hopes and dreams?

Old as they were, she and Dennis knew they couldn't be a family the way they'd been, but wouldn't it be fine to have balance back, some kind of father, a mother, two kids? Where did need fit into it, the competing needs alluded to by Ruby? Michelle failed to see how needing someone could be enough to keep that person in your life. Suppose the other didn't need to be needed. The thought scared her. Was that what had happened between her parents?

Here was Ruby at eighty brokenhearted over men she had loved, her mother happy for perhaps the first time in her fifties, and Molly—who knew if there was a man in her life unless it was some dead artist? Michelle wondered if she'd ever have time to meet anyone, law school so time-consuming that if you didn't have a significant other before you began, you could pretty much kiss the idea good-bye for years.

Ruby pushed a picture of Michelle and her parents across the table. Her mother, pregnant with Dennis, held a cigarette, but her father was holding Michelle and smiling. "You can keep that one," Ruby said. "Once upon a time," she began, then stopped. She opened and closed the album without another word.

The remnants of a floral arrangement, dry and shriveled now, sat on the mantel next to Ruby's Hummels. "Dead," Ruby said, staring at them. "Real pretty last week. Bea would never let them sit around like that."

Relieved to have something to do, Michelle dumped the dead flowers. Yuck. The scummy water was foul. She sprinkled Ajax in the sink, clearly untouched in days. She scooped a handful of raw rice into the vase, poured in some ammonia, and swished it around, as Bea had taught her years ago. She could take Ruby over to visit Bea, an excuse to get her out of that bathrobe, up and out of this house. Fresh air.

Maybe she needed it herself. Once upon a time, her parents had been happy together. At least the snapshot looked that way, but it reflected only a moment in time. If Michelle had learned anything in her first year of law school, it was not to draw a quick conclusion from slim evidence. Once upon a time didn't necessarily mean a happy ending. So much for precedent.

Ruby had always been glamorous, funny, the one who baked bourbon balls, not brownies, the one whose very presence made their family seem less conventional than it really was, but from Michelle's perspective, *safely* colorful. She'd never had the least idea of the complications Ruby had just confessed, and she was herself unprepared to comprehend love's unsuspected depths.

To love *one* person had proved too much for her. She and her high school boyfriend had not made it through sophomore year at college before going separate ways. The guy she dated after that had dumped her. Nobody she'd ever dated had moved her to such passion as Ruby had clearly wrestled with throughout her long life.

Michelle hoped this love-on-hold feeling was a temporary consequence of academic ambition; everyone she knew was so determined to make law review that long-range commitments weren't part of the picture. AIDS was real because of Frank, and between one thing and another, Michelle just plain wasn't ready to love someone, let alone some two.

Who would have suspected Ruby's predicament? This wasn't a big anonymous city, but a town where everybody knew everybody else, what kind of car they drove, where they bought groceries, who their families were or weren't. Never the kind of figure who could fade unobtrusively into the background, Ruby had nonetheless carried on— Michelle found herself shocked—Ruby and John Clay probably *did it* right up till the end.

Michelle kissed Ruby goodbye for the day. "Mama needs me for a little while," she said, and Ruby just hugged her and waved her away.

Now, Michelle took off for her grandmother's senior residence where surely her mother must be waiting among packing boxes by now. Poor Grandma. She had barely had time to settle into her new life before she'd left it. *Come and sit by my side if you love me.* Grandma had never sung that song. Never unkind, she'd never made demands, but neither had she engaged Michelle's attention as Ruby had. Had there been an unspoken need in Grandma that Michelle had missed? Too late, too late, she told herself. And anyway, what would a heaping of guilt do for anyone? Grandma was gone. What must Mama be feeling right now? To lose your mother, she could hardly imagine. Losing her father, even though he lived right here . . . oh, too hard to think about What if, whatever. She slowed down in the school crossing zone. What is the speed of love? The velocity of need? What kind of wreckage occurred when they collided, need like a patch of ice you didn't see on the road? Although Michelle wished she'd asked Ruby when she had the chance on that day at the beginning of summer, it would not have been right. Ruby probably didn't even remember what she'd said in her grief.

Michelle accelerated, speeding past the library half-buried in the shade of old magnolias, then the Arkansas Power and Light business office. A mile further on, she crossed the street where they had lived before the divorce, and she kept straight on until she got to Senior House—Death's Waiting Room, her mother called it. Elizabeth's car stood in the driveway, but as if to underscore the accuracy of her nickname for the place, a long black hearse from Stevens' Funeral Home was backing away, its curtain drawn.

God and the Devil

‿◯

"You picked a hell of a time to visit. I'm not dead yet. A tribute to the power of alcohol as a preservative," Ruby barked as I set down my luggage and crossed the bedroom to kiss her. Sitting up in bed, sallow rather than vibrant, my great-aunt wore a sateen bed jacket, quilted and speckled with spillage.

"Elizabeth won't even give me a drop of whiskey. I hope you brought some, Molly." I knew that grin, the flash of her eyes. The wobble of extra flesh at the chin was the only unfamiliar piece of her.

"You've only been home from the hospital for one day. Anyway, I thought you'd quit." I pulled the cherry desk chair toward the bed, noting the puffy fingers, the bruises on Ruby's arm where the hospital lab sticks had drawn blood.

"Girl, I did. I been sober *forever*, at least—I think it was—oh, who cares? Tell me what *you've* been up to lately, while I've gone and got myself sick. How's that wonderful man?"

"What wonderful man?" I replied. Ruby picked at her bed sheet as if she saw something on it. "I didn't fly all the way from California to tell you sad tales. I came to cheer you up."

"I am cheered," she said drily. "What happened? You seemed so happy."

"It was over months ago. Too good to be true." I sat there looking around her bedroom filled with sickroom paraphernalia. From their silver frames, her husband, Bubba, her lover, John Clay, and her nephew Frank, all dead, gazed back at the room as if they'd just walked into it and taken up positions of watchfulness.

I have thrown away pictures of recent joys, the formerly wonderful man and me in the Luxembourg gardens looking happier than anyone has a right to look at our age. On our wrists were antique watches purchased for one another on the Île St.-Louis, as if time past could be stopped, as if time present was all that mattered. Looking back, that was so; in fact we had no future.

"Remember how Elizabeth and I used to be so fascinated by Greek gods and goddesses when we were young?"

"Don't change the subject."

"We used to think of you as Persephone, going back and forth between worlds we didn't inhabit. You want to know what happened? I let down my guard. Swept up. I was *happy*." I pressed my hand against my upper lip to keep my voice steady. "And I never even saw it coming." She patted her lap, inclined her head toward me.

"Oh, darling," Ruby sighed. "Maybe he'll be back."

"I'm not holding my breath."

"How old is that devil?"

"Old enough to know better."

"Men. Some never do grow up," said Ruby. "Did I ever tell you that?"

"I'm not going to let it do me in."

"That's my girl." Ruby's eyes looked watered down. She squinted up at me from the pillows, stuck her lower lip way out, trying to make me smile. "You've lost some weight. It suits you. Too scrawny isn't good, though. Don't get carried away, Missy."

"Missy? I thought *I* was Missy." Elizabeth arrived with a tray of iced tea, mint in each glass.

"You're both Missy to me." Ruby sipped but was fretful. "Did I tell you John Clay put cable back here in the bedroom TV so he could watch golf matches without having to sit up in the front room . . . and then he—" Her voice snagged.

"Ruby," Elizabeth took her glass and set it on the nightstand just next to the lamp with the hand-painted roses on it. "Don't go getting yourself all upset again. We can tell Molly about it later. You rest awhile. I'm going to help her get settled. We'll be right here, or out in back. Just ring the bell if you need anything." She gestured toward the silver bell on the table by the bed, almost lost among the take-home items from the hospital, an emesis basin, swabs, a thermometer.

Through the bedroom windows the rose of Sharon ranged almost as high as the screens, filtering the light. Although Ruby's garden lay beyond it, we couldn't see it for all the foliage, but as we reached the door, she closed her eyes. "Pull the shades, make it darker please. Yes," she whispered, then was quiet.

Elizabeth and I hung my things next to hers in Ruby's guest room, the same room we used to share when we were invited for an overnight. The lamp between the beds was companion to the one in Ruby's room. I turned its switch to watch the painted roses glow, but nothing happened.

"Broken," my cousin said. "Last night I thought it needed a new bulb, but it's the switch." Against the wall at the foot of the bed hung something I hadn't seen before, an exuberant quilt, and before we went out to the back garden, I fingered it, admiring the varied triangles of men's shirting that ran in rows along the borders.

"Bubba's shirts, John Clay's too." At my shoulder Elizabeth pointed to merit badges in the intersections of red strips. "Frank's," she added, and I almost smelled airplane glue coming from the garage where Ruby's nephew made matchstick projects, where Bubba stored burlap bags of hard corn for his chickens, where dried lavender stalks hung upside down from the eaves, where filtered light used to fall on the rusting Dr. Pepper "10 2 4" sign on the wall between two wire-spoke wheels, the garage where I hid during games of hide-and-seek with our other cousins.

"Do you ever see any of the cousins? Do you ever think of those times at all?" I asked Elizabeth a few minutes later as we settled into the sunlit garden with our drinks.

"I can't even remember my first husband."

"Thank goodness they look like you," I said.

"Oh my God, yes. Imagine, especially with Dennis sitting across my breakfast table. He's gone now to Fayetteville, but when he's home for vacation, if he looked like his Daddy, I'd have a hard time not burning his toast, a harder time still just being—*nice*." Her dimples deepened as she grinned.

"What's Michelle up to?"

"Law school. Second year."

"What does Ruby have to say about that?"

"Say? She helps with tuition. Those two are close. When John Clay died last spring, Michelle came down to help her out some. Not having her own, Ruby's always taken on other people's kids. Even me. When Mama died, Ruby just moved over from being Ruby to almost-Mama, if you can imagine Mama with a sense of humor."

"Elizabeth, I'm sorry, truly sorry I wasn't here then."

"Don't think on it. I don't even go out to the cemetery myself. Can't think she's really there."

"It's hard being far away. Looking at Ruby's flowers, the garage, it's as if I never left, but Bubba's not coming home from the store, and she's so—frail."

After a moment, Elizabeth said, "People come to funerals for the damnedest reasons. Some, just because they don't have anything better to do. I ever tell you 'bout when Uncle Aaron passed? I was standing next to a man waiting to sign the book at the front of the funeral home in Memphis,

"'Did you know the deceased?' he asked.

"'Aaron was my grandfather's older brother,' I said. He said, 'I used to buy cotton from him. I come all the way from Conway, just to see whether the sonovabitch is really dead.'"

I laughed and spit at the same time, and now I looked like Ruby, spots all over my blouse. Although I dabbed at them with the paper napkin Elizabeth gave me with my drink, it was useless.

We sat and drank and swapped stories for a while, safer than bringing the conversation back around to my not being here for her mother's funeral. My aunt filed her tongue when most people brushed their teeth, and after our grandparents died, our families, separated by more than distance, never saw a lot of one another. I couldn't begin to think of a way to say this to Elizabeth.

I couldn't tell what she was thinking, another thing about just dropping out of the sky instead of living with people. You forget how to read their simplest intonations, although summers when we were young, we were practically telepathic, communicated with the slightest downturn of a lip, shrug of a shoulder, blink of an eyelash.

And although we fell back into a rare companionship, things were different now. We weren't gauging Grannie Maude's attitude toward Ruby, or Ruby's indifference to it. Grannie Maude has been gone since the week before my wedding, buried some twenty years ago in the silk print dress she was to have worn to it. Now we had to think about Ruby: it was her turn, but if she was ready, we were not.

We heard the unmistakable tinkle of Ruby's silver bell. "Oh, Lord," Elizabeth wheezed. We dashed for the back porch and slammed the screen door in our haste to get to her bedroom. It was hard to see coming in from the garden. I stumbled over an ottoman on my way into her room.

Ruby said, "I hate to be out of the loop. Heard you laughing out there. Do you have a joke for me?"

"Just being silly, talking about the dingbats and oddballs in this family," I said.

"This family is full of characters. I pale beside them," said Ruby, "and I am hardly the pastel type. Pour me a drink now, darling," she said in a voice that brooked no opposition. No percentage in denying her anything at this point.

"Let me fix you up a little for the cocktail hour." I pulled out a makeup mirror and lipstick while Elizabeth went for the whiskey. Ruby's hair had no luster, was lank, but still thick. With shaky hands she applied lipstick, smoothed her hair but wouldn't let me brush it.

"Maybe after my drink," she said. "It's not like there's anyone left to come visit." She looked hard at me. "When they die, you still get to love them."

She stared up at the photographs on the wall. "You get to love them so much they grow larger than life—unreal, to tell the truth. I expect there was a time when Bubba loomed bigger than anything in my life. And now I got John Clay floating up there too. Oh Lord, I need that drink."

She reached out her arms to me. "It's hard to stop loving someone. Not something I could ever do. Best I could do was try to stop seeing him when it got too complicated, love Bubba more, keep real busy. But when Bubba died, John Clay and I took up again. You know we were sweethearts long before I ever met Bubba? So many good years."

When Elizabeth returned to the bedroom with the whiskey and three glasses, my head was buried in Ruby's lap and I was sobbing, a sorry sight, a tangle of linen and grief. "Oh, honey," she said, and patted me on the part of me she could reach, my butt.

Ruby smoothed my hair back around my ear, like she used to do when I was little and Elizabeth and I spent the night at her house. How long we stayed like that I don't know, but I heard crickets singing when I lifted my head from the pillows. Ruby was asleep. Elizabeth's chair was empty, and I heard cooking noises in the kitchen, the scrape of spoon against skillet.

"I was thinking," Elizabeth said when I entered the room, "we could get together maybe once a year.

Even if we did it, and we won't, maybe three or four days a year, and maybe healthy enough for another twenty-five years to pull it off; do the math. We'd spend, at a maximum, one hundred days together. It doesn't seem like a lot, does it?"

"You remind me of Grannie Maude: numbers, measuring."

"And you are more like Ruby—not keeping track," she answered, somewhat severely. "She is just awful about her medication. She will tell you she's the only one whose system for counting out the pills is any good, next minute she'll complain that she has only white pills, and why in the name of God can't they make some of them different colors so a person can know without a magnifying glass which one is which."

The vision of Ruby counting out morning and evening doses, her hand shaking, her eyesight not what it used to be, but her stubborn streak undiminished by age or ill health, stopped me mid-kitchen. Instead of heading toward the refrigerator, I moved to the range, attempted giving Elizabeth a hug, but she shrugged her shoulders.

"Tell you what, Elizabeth: one hundred days is not enough. Let's make a pact like we used to do, and try hard not to break it. Every year, no matter what, let's plan a week someplace. California; Chicago; Branson, Missouri—it doesn't matter where. We could even go to London or Europe."

"For a *week*?"

"You always were the practical one. If we cross an ocean, two weeks."

"What if we get married again?" she asked.

"What if we do? They can come with us, or stay home. Or if they are old and sick or we are, then we can just visit one another where we live."

"It sounds good," she said doubtfully.

"I have so many travel miles from work," I said suddenly shy about this. Would it seem like bragging? "We could use some of them and go off to Europe. If I don't use the miles, they just expire. You'd be doing me a favor. Also," I said, full of benign intentions, "while I'm here, I can help organize some of Ruby's clutter, paperwork. Is the store sold? Is it rented out? Are her affairs in order?"

"John Clay helped her some. I don't know how up-to-date her papers are. He was just wonderful to her, Molly. Even riding Beatrice home at the end of the day, I guess you know this—that's when it happened, his heart attack, when he was taking Bea home from Ruby's, after work."

"No, I didn't know. How's Bea? Was she hurt?"

"Half-dead herself; had to quit working altogether. That's why I had to move over here for a little while. Bea's too weak herself, even before the accident, but especially now. It's only been five months. I'm surprised you didn't know."

Bea had worked for Ruby as long as I could remember, more than forty years. I heard an undertone of reproach beneath Elizabeth's surprise.

"Why didn't Ruby ever marry John Clay?" I asked.

"Not for lack of love. I don't know. Ask her."

"Ask her? Girl, do I look that stupid? No, you."

"No, you." Elizabeth waved the spatula in my direction.

You. You. We fell into the words as if we were ten again, but I felt each of us asking ourself if we would marry again, and if so, what it would take. Is the idea of dying alone without anyone around so terrible that I'd marry for the companionship?

"This is great," I said.

"It is great," said Elizabeth, forgiveness in her voice. "We just have to redefine great."

She splashed brandy over the chicken livers. "I got whipped potatoes staying warm in the stove, there. I'm fixing to heat us some greens; then we'll be all ready for supper. Ruby loves greens, and I can get her to sprinkle vinegar on them, no backfat, no bacon."

Greens. Vinegar. Backfat or bacon. Greens. Vinegar, cornbread and butter. The music of it, the sound of it. The feel of Ruby's fingers smoothing my hair behind my ear, a tangible lullaby, it's no wonder I felt years fall away.

Elizabeth couldn't possibly read my mind, but she said, "It *is* like being kids again, having you here, only we're old enough to do the cooking, and Bubba's gone, as if he's still at the store."

"No Bubba, no David or Marilee. It's as if the cousins are just distant as usual, off in Ohio, just not here. Some kind of joke: now you see them, now you don't."

"No joking at David's funeral, that's for sure. Not ever when anyone young dies, let alone with the whole world watching and praying." Elizabeth set the lid over the skillet and turned off the heat.

"Did you go up to Cleveland for his funeral?" I asked.

"No, Michelle was just born; well, I don't have to tell you," she said, her dimple deepening a fraction. She really did seem to have let something go.

"Elizabeth, this is how far away I've been: back in 1972 when it happened, I heard descriptions about the Olympics, especially about the American who'd made aliyah to Israel so he could be a weightlifter in the Olympics. To myself I was thinking, What kind of a Jewish boy is that?—sort of amused; this was *before*. Later, after the terror began—they were still in the Olympic Village at that point— I was driving home from the market praying with everybody. When I got home, Mama called to say that was *our* David, Dorothy's son. I hadn't had the slightest idea.

"I saw Uncle Bubba on the nightly news escorting his body back. My folks flew up to Cleveland for the funeral, and they told me about Aunt Sarah and Aaron. Imagine grandparents losing a grandchild. Those images on TV. The stocking-masked terrorist on the balcony mixed with memories of tiger lilies in Ruby's garden and all of us little kids playing there, the helicopter blowing up, horrible, horrible."

Elizabeth took food out of the oven. "How could you say to anyone, 'that's part of our family' without trading on the loss? I couldn't tell anyone. Most people knew, of course, a town this size. David could spit watermelon seeds farther than anyone else."

"He learned to ride a two-wheeler one summer before I did. Could you say that to a living soul? I couldn't," I said.

She turned. "Use these pot holders for the greens. That dish is hot."

The bell rang again.

"What does a person have to do to get a little attention?" Ruby asked. "I smell chicken livers. I smell greens. Also, I almost forgot, Little Stevens is coming by later. I will put on more lipstick. We need more light, more light in here."

"Little?"

"Old Mr. Stevens been dead for years, not long after your Daddy Doc died."

"Mama didn't let me come. Thought I was too young." Elizabeth shot me a look, but not mean.

"Colored stood all around the funeral home that day to pay their respects to your grandfather, the only doc in town who'd treat them. Old Mr. Stevens wouldn't let them in. Little buries everybody now, if they've got the money. Times change," Ruby said. "By the time Bubba died, everybody who wanted to could come into the service. He would have liked that. 'Course, it wasn't a mob scene. A shopkeeper isn't the same as a doctor."

"Funerals aren't contests."

"There were more than a hundred people at Bubba's funeral," added Elizabeth.

Ruby continued as if she hadn't heard either of us. "We like to have had us some real trouble when Frank died though. Now they treat AIDS like they used to do color. Like they could catch it by being human. Still, Little Stevens handled everything fine. It was just that idiot who answers the phone made a fuss at first."

"Why is he coming by?" Elizabeth ventured.

"Some last-minute arrangement to take care of. No point in leaving it to you two. But maybe you'll want to know ahead of time so it won't shock you."

What could shock us? By then we had TV trays set up in her bedroom, a bed tray for Ruby; we all tucked into the chicken livers. Ruby shook the vinegar cruet and looked over its faceted sides with a half-smile.

"After John Clay's accident," she paused, and her face drained of color, "at the funeral home, his daughters came over from Memphis to make arrangements. Of course over the years I had met them, but it wasn't exactly as if we were best friends. It wasn't like I had official standing. But he wanted to be cremated, not buried, and they went along." After a long pause, she put down the cruet.

After another moment she said, slyly, "I made me an arrangement with Little Stevens. He's coming tonight to discuss it; I don't want you to be surprised."

Elizabeth and I looked at each other, eyebrows slightly elevated.

"He saved me a portion of John Clay's ashes, out of the urn he gave the family." She looked over to the far wall, where her dresser held an array of photographs, perfume bottles, and general clutter. "That marble thing there, that box—" she waved. "It's alabaster, a peach. We got it in Mexico, a few years ago. Nothing special, but it comes apart," she said.

I picked it up. It did. Inside was a little Baggie full of ashes. "It's a goddamn reliquary," I said, not knowing whether to laugh or cry.

"I got me a strand of what hair Bubba had left at the end," she said, "in the envelope in the drawer of my jewelry box. And when I go into the ground, I want both of them with me. I can give them to Stevens tonight, or you can tuck 'em in when you kiss me goodbye."

"Oh, Ruby," I began, "you'll still be around for awhile." She'd barely touched her food. Even her drink was still sitting there. She shook her head.

"Only reason I'm still alive, darlin', God and the devil are fighting over who gets me. Doesn't either one of 'em really want me, too much trouble. But sooner or later they'll have more to do than fight over me," she grinned. "Whoever loses gets me."

"What do *you* want, Ruby?"

"I trust y'all a damn sight more than Stevens. Only I don't want anyone else knowing nothing about it. It's private." Elizabeth and I remained smooth-countenanced right up until the moment she furrowed her forehead to figure out just where these souvenirs of Bubba and John Clay would rest in that final resting place, her medium-priced, satin-lined coffin.

Then, while Ruby thought out loud about the possibilities, we lost our composure, cracked, snorted with the effort of concealing chuckles. Keeping a straight face was impossible for either of us as Ruby said, "My hands will be folded with some damned dahlias in them, so why not just slip that lock of Bubba's hair into my own hair, and as for John Clay, you girls will just have to figure it out when the time requires it of you."

Elizabeth reached for a tissue to blow her nose as Ruby considered where to put John Clay's ashes—at her shoulder, her ankles, or somewhere in between since he'd spent so much of his active life there anyway—"I just want Little Stevens to know you know, that you have my permission, nothing written down."

Later, we lay on our beds laughing until we ached with the effort of it.

"No wonder she and Grannie Maude didn't get along in this world. Maybe not the next one either," I said.

Elizabeth propped herself up on her elbow and looked across at me. "Molly," she asked, "do Jewish people believe in an afterlife?"

"You mean officially, or do I?" I couldn't say that what I thought was anything but idiosyncratic. "I don't really believe in any life but this one. What about you?"

Elizabeth said, "Mama always maintained that she was Jewish herself, right up until Grannie Maude and Daddy Doc died, but she never went to services. She never forgave the rabbi over in Helena for refusing to officiate at her wedding. Sent all of us to Daddy's church. Why, she asked, would she drive forty-five miles to educate her children as Jews when the marriage hadn't been sanctioned by that holier-than-thou? They had to call Daddy's Methodist minister the morning of the wedding to drive over to perform the service."

"That's why half my cousins are Jewish and half Methodist, because of the rabbi?" I sat straight up. "I'd always thought your parents just didn't feel like driving so far to a temple when the church was just down the street." I didn't mention my parents' theory that Sunday morning hangovers had also been a deciding factor.

"It was more than convenience. Imagine, all the excitement of your wedding day shadowed by last-minute censure, having to scramble for a clergy-man. Even Grannie Maude never criticized Mama for doing what she did. We knew were Jewish, half, anyway, but never knew what to believe. Neither she nor Daddy cared for organized religion, or orga-nized anything." Elizabeth looked over at me. "But what if there is some celestial or subterranean space, and Ruby turns up wherever place, with Bubba and John Clay standing there in attendance?"

"If you mean do I imagine them all meeting up again, "I said, "I vote an emphatic *no*. And if you think I have any idea where to put those ashes, no again."

"But we promised—"

"I don't mean we won't do it."

"Are you saying that you're going to stay a while?"

"Ummm. Yes."

"Ummm. Good." Elizabeth continued as if she didn't want to give me a chance to change my mind. "Here's what I think: the afterlife—Mama's not here, but she's not exactly what I'd call gone. Some-times I catch myself thinking of something funny about her . . . watching my kids drive her old car, I remember things I want to tell her, and it's hard. Difficult as she was, it's hard."

"Do you imagine her sitting around in Heaven drinking with her friends or your Daddy?" Even as I spoke it sounded stupid, but being here in Ruby's familiar house with Elizabeth evoked a time when we spent many evenings like this puzzling out life's lessons, its meaning, one's place in the universe, with or without understanding. Elizabeth didn't seem to mind my foolish question.

"I don't imagine her out at the cemetery. Can't even see her able to breathe without her oxygen. I try to imagine her laughing."

"Laughing. Yes."

She rolled over on one side facing me across the space between our beds, one arm propping her head, hand under her chin. "Still, you, not half-Jewish, half-Methodist, Arkansas variety blend, but 100 percent Jewish, religious school and temple in the same town you lived in, tons of Jewish kids to grow up with—what do you believe? I remember we came up to St. Louis once for your Daddy's birthday, and it was that harvest festival with all the vegetables and fruit up on the altar at the temple, and a little shed made out of branches. Did all that celebrating have anything to do with life after death? Being good so you could go to Heaven and not just get to stay out later at night?"

Elizabeth was closer to me than my own sister. It struck me as evasive to veer off into another area that interested me, that Christians *thank* God, but Jews *praise* God. This had nothing to do with the afterlife, but with one's relation to the deity, if one believed. In spite of myself I began to think of paintings from the museum where I worked—on canvas, arms upraised, praise looked like thanks, looked like supplication. It seemed very hard for me, and very distant from my life, to come up with any satisfactory answers. Earlier, Ruby had joked about God and the Devil. Or was she joking?

The sukkah Elizabeth remembered, the festival booth, probably looked a lot like Thanksgiving minus the Pilgrims. *Celebrating*, the word she'd used. Yes, Jews celebrated life, not death. But was that an answer, or another evasion? I finally answered.

"I've spent so much of my life wondering whether there's life *before* death—that difficult marriage, trying to figure out what I was doing wrong, trying to please someone with no capacity for joy—that I haven't formed an opinion, let alone held a belief, about what comes next. Elizabeth, I haven't even made plans for my own—demise. I don't own a cemetery plot, haven't decided whether to be buried or cremated."

"Girl, we're only fifty. Neither have I!" Elizabeth began to chew on the plastic straw again.

"Do you think Ruby is just more practical, or did she *get* practical because she's—" I couldn't make myself say it aloud, not even to Elizabeth. "I think of myself as extremely practical, but . . ."

"You are not extremely—that. You're more like a grasshopper than an ant, or maybe a bird, not a squirrel. You prepare for what's happening now, operate on a need-to-know basis. No, I'm not criticizing." Elizabeth waved her chewed straw around in the air at the expression on my face. "It's your temperament. I'm more like an ant. I know it. Or the little red hen, that goody-two-shoes. Damn, I hated that chicken."

"It's not bad to be organized the way you are."

"Girl, don't lie to me. It's just my temperament. You don't get points, when all's said and done, for being one way or another. Not unless there *is* an afterlife and it turns out to be run by accountants."

"Tomorrow let's ask Ruby what she thinks about it."

"Isn't that kind of tacky, asking now?"

"When might there be another chance?"

We lay side by side thinking our own private thoughts; then Elizabeth looked at her watch.

"Time for Ruby's medicine. I hate waking her up to take pills to help her sleep."

"Stay put, I'll do it," I said, but when I padded barefoot down the hall, Ruby was awake watching Jay Leno with the mute button on. I raised an eyebrow questioning, and she said "I'm practicing."

"For what?"

"John Clay and I went to New York a couple of years ago. I wanted to go to the opera, like Cher in *Moonstruck*. Didn't understand a word. Loved it. Made up my own words for what they might be saying to one another, Butterfly and that bastard Pinkerton. That's what I'm doing now. More interesting than whatever those clowns are talking about." She waved toward the television.

I picked up the segmented pill box marked PM. "You're practicing for your next opera?"

"I'm practicing *goodbye*." Ruby stared from the pillows. "For a smart girl, you aren't always too swift, sugar. Still, I'm glad you've come. See, I've got hello down pretty well. Goodbyes are harder. I haven't stopped looking for John Clay to walk right through that door. Did I tell you?"

"Elizabeth did. It's awful." I stepped close and smoothed Ruby's hair from her forehead, stroking it. "Plain unmitigated awful, and Bea flat on her back too. The quilt you two made is . . ." I searched for the right word.

"Wild Goose Chase," she whispered, closing her eyes.

"You're tired. Swallow these, and I'll turn out the lights."

"Goose," she whispered, squeezing my hand as I stood by the black walnut bed casting back to summers when Elizabeth and I spent the night here, when Ruby took out her manicure tray to paint our fingers and toes, telling us stories as she lifted each hand. Mostly her stories were about things that could happen in the future, accompanied by instructions to help us through events which, unlikely as it seemed then, could, would, happen to us.

"You will marry," Ruby had predicted. "You will have children," she told Elizabeth.

"You will travel far," she told me, and then years fell away and I was sitting at Ruby's kitchen table, one hand soaking in a bowl of soapy water, the other spread out on a folded towel as Ruby took an orange stick and pushed at my ragged cuticles.

"Will I be happy when I grow up?"

"That, sugar, is up to you," Ruby said, squeezing my hand, and then I was back in the room with the paraphernalia of illness, the thermometer, the chart on which we checked off dosages, what and when. No scent of nail polish remover or nail polish, but faint antiseptic smells.

Ruby used to keep a Ouija board for our visits, complete with predictions, certain answers that came up, no matter how crazy the questions. Answers remote as stars. That certainty—how had it eroded over the years? How, at an age when I'm supposed to know things, know them from experience, do I feel tentative as a dragonfly hovering over a pond, flitting, not designed for landing, never coming to a resting place? Is my life a skimming bird's life, am I a goose, a blackbird singing *Where somebody waits for me, sugar's sweet, so is she . . . Blackbird, bye-bye*?

"Goose," Ruby said again, pushing herself halfway up the layered pillows at her back. "Wild Goose Chase—it's the name of the quilt pattern Bea and I used. All those triangles like geese in autumn heading for the great beyond."

"*Is* there a great beyond, Ruby?"

"If there is, and there's long-distance dialing, I'll let you know. No, I'm being silly; forgive me, darling. Truth is, I believe there's here and now, and maybe tomorrow, but I'm not a very good example. I've spent my life a day at a time, not hoarding it up for any future payoff. Made more than a few bad investments, hit some jackpots, get to die in my own bed, you here, and Elizabeth, but Bubba, John Clay, Frank, all gone before me. Gone. And gone is gone except in someone's memory. Long as you remember me, that's my afterlife, sugar pie."

"That's very Jewish, that thought. You know that?"

"Maybe I got it by osmosis, forty-plus years married to Bubba. You recall your great-grandmother at all, Miss Sissie?"

"No more than an image of her sitting on her front porch glider, or turning the dial when they got that television. The Indian face on the test screen pattern, I remember that, how we all sat and stared at it. That's clearer than her face."

"Bubba and Doc bought her that television together. First one in town. She made life hell for me at first, but after a while we made some peace. Miss Sissie wouldn't let your Grannie Maude set foot in her house until your mama was born, even though Maude had converted before she married Doc. Later, when I heard that, I figured that's why Bubba wanted to elope. Wasn't going to do me any good being Jewish or not, not in Miss Sissie's eyes. Still, Bubba was her youngest; she doted on him. And he wouldn't visit her unless he could bring me along, so she had a different set of rules for me than she'd laid down for Maude."

"Seems like everybody had a different set of rules for you, Ruby, long as I can remember."

She continued as if I hadn't said a word. "I'd be sitting there on her scratchy red horsehair sofa listening to them talk. That old woman would always sneak in something about the Bible. First, I thought it was foreign, she'd say 'the Persia this week,' yada yada, and I never could figure out what she was going on about. Then Bubba, driving home from his mother's house one day, asked what I thought about when we visited, and I said whenever she goes on about Persia, I think about Aladdin and Ali Baba, stuff like that. He laughed so hard I thought he'd drive that car right into a field.

"'*Parsha*, not Persia,' he sort of gasped, and I asked him where was *Parsha*, Mr. Smarty Pants, and he said all this time his mama had been trying to give me Jewish instruction, talking about the part of the Bible that came up for reading that week, called the *parsha*. Now, Miss Molly, how in the world was a country girl like me to know that?"

We grinned at one another. Ruby began to cough, and took some water. "I haven't thought of that stuff in years," she said. "Whatever Jewish I got, I got it from her, 'cause Bubba sure in hell didn't talk about such things as life after death. We had us a good life. No children; that was a heartache. Still, we had Frank, my sister's son. Once in a while, summers, we had you girls on loan. You make do." She rubbed her temples and eyes, then fished around for the remote, clicked off the television.

"I'm very sleepy all of a sudden." Her eyes fluttered shut, her hands quiet on the counterpane. "Maybe it's all a goose chase," I thought she whispered as I stood looking down at her, chilled as if she'd taken flight. *Make my bed and light the light. I'll be home late tonight. Blackbird, bye-bye.* But where would Ruby fly? Toward what or to whom? And when she went, where would home be now?

I ran down the hall to get Elizabeth. From either side of Ruby's bed we dodged around lamps and medicine; we bent to kiss her. All our lives we had worshiped Ruby. I couldn't imagine either of us fighting over her as we'd both got plenty of attention from our childless great-aunt. But she'd never paid a lick of attention, so far as I knew, to either God or the devil. Had I been a believer, it would not have been too hard to imagine them as she'd predicted, wrestling now for her company, her great and generous soul.

4-14
d